Dear Reader:

LOVESWEPT celebrates  who sweep us off our feet, endearments, and who c humor and hidden vulnera roughnecks or dashing sop and danger- ous or blond and brash, these men are heartthrobs, the kind no woman can get enough of. And now, just in time for Valentine's Day, all six books in this month's line-up have truly special covers that feature only these gorgeous heartthrobs. HEARTTHROBS—heroes who'll leave you spellbound as only real men can, in six fabulous new romances by only the best in the genre.

Don't miss any of our HEARTTHROBS this month

#528 A MAGNIFICENT AFFAIR by Fayrene Preston
#529 CALL ME SIN by Jan Hudson
#530 MR. PERFECT by Doris Parmett
#531 LOVE AND A BLUE-EYED COWBOY
        by Sandra Chastain
#532 TAKEN BY STORM by Tami Hoag
#532 BRANDED by Linda Warren

There's no better way to celebrate the most romantic day of the year than to cuddle up with all six LOVESWEPT HEARTTHROBS!

With best wishes,

Nita Taublib

Nita Taublib
Associate Publisher/LOVESWEPT

WHAT ARE *LOVESWEPT* ROMANCES?

They are stories of true romance and touching emotion. We believe those two very important ingredients are constants in our highly sensual and very believable stories in the *LOVESWEPT* line. Our goal is to give you, the reader, stories of consistently high quality that may sometimes make you laugh, sometimes make you cry, but are always fresh and creative and contain many delightful surprises within their pages.

Most romance fans read an enormous number of books. Those they truly love, they keep. Others may be traded with friends and soon forgotten. We hope that each *LOVESWEPT* romance will be a treasure—a "keeper." We will always try to publish

LOVE STORIES YOU'LL NEVER FORGET
BY AUTHORS YOU'LL ALWAYS REMEMBER

The Editors

Loveswept ® 533

Linda Warren
Branded

BANTAM BOOKS
NEW YORK · TORONTO · LONDON · SYDNEY · AUCKLAND

BRANDED

A Bantam Book / March 1992

*If you would be interested in receiving protective vinyl
covers for your Loveswept books, please write to this address
for information:*

> *Loveswept*
> *Bantam Books*
> *P.O. Box 985*
> *Hicksville, NY 11802*

ISBN 0-553-44208-2

Published simultaneously in the United States and Canada

PRINTED IN THE UNITED STATES OF AMERICA

OPM   0 9 8 7 6 5 4 3 2 1

AUTHOR'S NOTE:

Rodeo fans may notice that I've taken some liberties with the scheduling of actual rodeos mentioned in this book. The changes were made for the purposes of fiction, and with all due respect to the cowboys, cowgirls, and their families who have to accommodate their lives to the real schedules.

Branded

One

Tanner Danielson hit the dirt, face first.

He heard a sympathetic, disappointed moan from the crowd in the arena, as a sharp pain jabbed his ribs and he tasted rodeo dust between his teeth.

"Keep it down, please, folks," the PA squawked. "Let the medics do their jobs."

Tanner rolled over, eyes shut, then raised himself out of the dust on his elbows, wiped a hand across his dirt-smeared face, and waved off the medics.

A video camera stared at him, held on the shoulder of a burly, gray-haired cameraman. Beside the man, one slim hand holding a microphone bearing the letters KVCD-TV, was the woman Tanner had gone to jail for thirteen years ago. He hadn't been within a mile of her since then, but there was no question of who she was. Shoulder-length, sunlight-and-honey blond hair, fair skin, that way of standing so still, he'd swear time had stopped—she hadn't changed enough to make a damn bit of difference in his reaction to her since the first day he'd met her. She'd been beautiful, vulnerable . . . and his best friend's wife.

One glimpse of her had been enough to wreak havoc on his concentration and his eight-second ride.

He swore.

The wide-set gold-flecked brown eyes, so innocent they should be outlawed, were fixed on his face in an unblinking, unreadable stare. But her throat worked as she swallowed convulsively, and that small betrayal of emotion wrenched through Tanner's gut with a force that made his fall seem like Sunday afternoon backyard antics.

Adrenaline got him to his feet before he could assess the damage to his ribs. He clenched his teeth shut on another curse and bent over to pick up his hat.

A wave of applause started in the stands at the announcer's urging. "Let's hear it, folks. Your applause is the only pay this cowboy's going to get today."

What kind of perverse fate had brought Julie Fielding to a rodeo he was riding in? And what kind of perverse fascination had made him look at her?

He jammed his hat onto his head and closed his eyes for a moment, testing his ribs with a shallow breath. His reaction to Julie Fielding was predictable as hell—she made every masculine nerve in his body forget that his brain cells were supposed to be in charge. She always had.

The video camera was still aimed at him when he looked at it again. So were the wide brown eyes. Pride stiffened Tanner's spine. He limped toward her. Three feet away he stopped. A tiny frown line marked her forehead. It hadn't been there thirteen years ago. Her face was more finely drawn now, the bone structure more apparent.

The big gray-haired cameraman beside her was fiddling with his equipment, obviously excusing himself from the exchange.

His expression hard, Tanner raised his hand to his hat. "I apologize for the short ride," he said, courtesy laid on as thick as the dirt. "Ma'am."

Her eyebrows arched in surprise, and finally she murmured, "Sometimes they're short for everyone." Her hair swung slightly around her face, apparently impervious to dust. He'd forgotten just how much her hair could make a cowboy want to reach out and run his fingers through it.

Tanner checked the impulse, then noticed the almost imperceptible whitening of her knuckles and had a fleeting picture of Julie the way she'd once been. Too young for the troubles she was facing, too stubborn and proud to ask for help, too wary of him to let him offer.

"Yeah, sometimes they're short for everyone," he said, staring at her, irritated by the memory. "But you don't always get the pleasure of watching 'em again on the evening news."

Her chin went up a notch. "You won't get the pleasure tonight either," she said brusquely. "It's not for the news."

"What's it for, then?" he asked, when it was clear she wasn't going to explain.

"A six-week project."

The muscles in his chest tightened. *A six-week project?* Did that mean she was going to be around for a while? He studied her, wondering about the implications of that. Wondering how he'd handle the idea of Julie Fielding watching all his rides, with those brown eyes that reflected every emotion she felt and that attitude of cool distance she thought she gave off.

"You hoping for more pictures of how to bite the dust?" he said shortly.

"I wasn't *hoping* for this one," she said.

"Yeah. I didn't intend to oblige you either. *Ma'am*." He touched his hand to his hat. "Don't count on it again."

"Tanner," she said, when he started to turn away. "I'm sorry about the fall. I . . . we wouldn't use that footage without your permission."

The big cameraman shot a sharp, skeptical look toward Julie, and an edge of grim amusement lifted one corner of Tanner's mouth. Permission, hell. Burly Shoulders didn't intend to miss his chances. "Yeah," Tanner said. "Write me a note on white stationery. Make sure you say please." He stepped away from the press corral and turned toward the rails beyond the chutes.

Julie Fielding wasn't going to write him any notes. She never had. Not even to answer the letters he'd written to her after Buck's funeral. As if he didn't have the right to speak to Buck's widow. The judgment had rankled all the more because it was unfair. He'd never as much as touched her, around the arena or anyplace else. She'd been off-limits, and Tanner had accepted that. He'd never been alone with her in a place where any of the things he thought about could happen. He'd needed every barrier she could put up.

Now that Buck was gone, maybe he still did.

Halfway through his painful progress across the dirt, he heard the whir of the video camera.

Lens trained on the cowboy, Nick Johnson

stayed with the shot for a full ten seconds, then glanced toward his partner.

Meeting his gaze, Julie realized she was standing with the microphone dangling limply from her fingers, staring at Tanner Danielson's exit, and saying not a single word on tape.

Nick turned off the video recorder and grinned at her. "So, partner. You're a friend of Tanner Danielson." His grin widened. "Top contender for the title, ex-con, a man with a past, and you've got connections with him. Pay dirt, kiddo."

She held his gaze for a moment, then her eyes flicked back to the cowboy climbing the rails.

Thirteen years. But just looking at him, she could have been eighteen again—broke, desperate, married to the wrong man . . . knowing she'd be better off if she'd never set eyes on Tanner Danielson, yet unable to look away from him, unable to stop picturing his face in front of her even while she was sitting through Buck's funeral. The memory made her fingers tighten around the mike cord. "I don't know if *friend* is the word, Nick," she said.

Nick ignored the tone of her voice, caught up in professional possibilities. "Whatever. Get the interview."

Julie shook her head. "What makes you think he's going to talk to me?"

"That fall just cost him three thousand bucks, and maybe the national title when they tally everything up at the end of the season. Every viewer in the world is going to want to know what your blue-eyed cowboy has to say about it."

She let out a breath, admitting he was right with an unconvincing protest. "I don't even know if he'll still be in town after this rodeo, Nick," she muttered.

"Check his room, or his trailer, or wherever he's staying."

"Wherever it is, he won't be there. *If* he's still in town, he'll be at the same local watering hole every other cowboy in town is at."

"Some cowboy bar?"

Julie glanced back at him. "In this town it's the Hoof and Horn. The beer's cheap, and they don't serve sushi."

Nick nodded, amused. "You want me to go with you?"

Julie met the level gaze in silence. It was an unrealistic offer. She'd been a reporter long enough to know you didn't set up a difficult interview with a camera at your elbow.

She'd asked to work with Nick on this documentary. A tough, experienced independent cameraman, he brought skill and energy to the project. What he expected from her was a personal connection to her Seattle TV station . . . and to the rodeo world.

More to the point, what she expected from herself was the kind of grit it would take to face Tanner Danielson on her own.

"No," she said finally. "You don't have to come with me. I've been in cowboy bars before."

He didn't make any of the cynical comments her statement could have drawn.

He didn't have to, Julie thought. She was making them all to herself.

The Hoof and Horn was raucous, noisy, and full of cowboys either celebrating their victories or drowning their disappointment. Julie stood just inside the door for a moment, adjusting to the dim light, the cigarette smoke, the smell of beer and saddle leather, the whiskey-rough voice of a country-and-western singer pulsing out of the jukebox.

The music hadn't changed much since she'd been there last. Nor had the cowboys—arrogant, unapologetically macho, charming their women with cowboy chivalry and devil-may-care grins while they did exactly as they pleased. Julie wondered how many of the women there were young wives or long-term girlfriends, trying to talk their men into leaving before the place closed, looking at the grim choice of a night in a bar or another long evening alone in a trailer or cheap motel room, wondering whose company had taken their place.

She shrugged off the memory of the many times she'd been in exactly the same situation, walked in, and took an empty stool at the bar.

"What'll it be, ma'am?" the bartender asked.

"Beer—whatever's on draft," she told him.

And Tanner Danielson. On tape, agreeing to an interview. She closed her eyes and pressed a hand to her rib cage for a moment, fighting for the composure she usually took for granted. Thirteen years. But seeing him in the arena this afternoon . . . it could have been yesterday. He'd looked the same as he had when he was twenty-two: tall and lean, with a cowboy's tanned face, and a level, too-direct blue gaze. And a tendency to be a little too honest.

Tanner Danielson, contender for Cowboy of the Year, in the top ten for the past three seasons. He must be making the kind of money Buck had always dreamed about. She wondered what he was doing with it. High living? Hand-tooled boots? A new Coupe de Ville?

None of those had been Tanner's style. An image formed in her memory, suddenly and without warning: Tanner Danielson in worn jeans, scuffed boots, and plain shirt, standing in a motel room in Helena, where he'd just carried Buck home and dumped him on the bed. For a few seconds, with Buck in his rodeo finery unconscious between them, Tanner had given her one of his looks— straight from the hip, dangerously male—that had sent shivers down her spine.

"Here you go." The bartender returned with her beer. Julie dragged her attention back to where she was, paid the man, and sipped from the glass, postponing the moment she'd have to look around her.

She was thirty-one, a rising reporter at KVCD, mortgage-holder of a well-maintained three-bedroom Cape Cod house in suburban Seattle, the mother of a bright, healthy thirteen-year-old who took piano lessons and played soccer. The thought of Skye steadied her.

Skye—the immeasurably good result of a bad choice, who salved all regrets—was the reason she was here. She hated working on the road, but if she and Nick made a success of this documentary, she had every chance of being promoted to special-programs director. The position offered a raise and another measure of security, and Julie wanted it. Needed it. If she had to face her ghosts to get it, she would. Maybe it was time, anyway, to face her ghosts. Before Skye got old enough to recognize them.

She felt a prickling at the back of her neck, as if

she was being stared at. She ignored it for half a minute, then gave in and glanced behind her.

Tanner Danielson was leaning against the stand-up counter at the far wall. He was flanked by two young women who were attractive, smiling, obviously interested, but he'd been staring a hole in the back of Julie's head.

Tanner watched Julie's brown eyes widen as her gaze met his. She sat perfectly still for a moment, looking back at him, one hand resting against the column of her neck under her hair. Then she blinked, set her beer down carefully on the bar, got up from the stool, and started across the room in his direction.

Tanner felt a kick of surprise. Thirteen years ago Julie Fielding wouldn't have sought him out. Thirteen years ago she'd been married.

The redhead on Tanner's right leaned a little closer, brushing his arm as she reached for her beer, but Tanner's attention didn't waver from Julie Fielding.

Her hair gleamed with reflections from the bar lights as she moved. Her face, her walk, the white chinos and loose, pale gold sweater, the subtle reserve that said her emotions weren't available at the request of some cowboy who might want to tap them, made her stand out in the rough atmosphere of the bar like a lily in the desert. She didn't belong in this crowd. She never had.

From the jukebox, Jesse Adam Wilson's smoky voice crooned, "I took one look at you, and I fell hard," and Tanner's mouth curved at one corner. He doubted that Jesse had fallen as hard as he had, but then, Jesse hadn't been on a mean bronc in a rodeo arena.

"Hello." She smiled at him.

He touched his fingers to the brim of his hat and nodded, feeling an edge of sexual awareness like the explosive heat of good whiskey. "Julie."

"It's been a while, Tanner," she said.

He studied her face. "Counting the last time, it's been about four hours," he said, drawling sarcastically to counter the growing heaviness in the lower part of his body.

She smiled again, ducking her head and running her hand along the side of her neck. The graceful gesture held a trace of nervousness, and it made her look younger. "Well, since I saw you ride . . ."

"You didn't see me ride. You saw me falling off."

The redhead leaning against his right arm laughed a little too appreciatively and rested her hand on Tanner's shoulder, staking her claim.

Julie's glance took in the gesture. When she looked at him again, it was with wry understanding. "Well, I don't plan to take up your whole evening, but—"

"How much of it do you plan to take up?"

"Well, no more than it takes to listen to a song on the jukebox," she said smoothly. "All right?"

"You asking me to dance?" The question was out before he could consider what would happen if she said yes. But, he realized with practiced self-awareness, he would have asked it anyway. He'd dreamed too often of Julie Fielding walking across a bar toward him, smiling at him, going home with him instead of Buck. When had his reaction to her ever been anything he could control?

She blinked, drew in a quick breath, lifted her chin, and said, "Yes."

Tanner studied her for several seconds, evaluating his emotions, then pushed himself away from the counter. He murmured, "Excuse me," to the woman leaning on his shoulder, and put his hand on Julie's back to steer her to the dance floor.

As they made their way through the crowd, the song on the jukebox changed to an upbeat piece of Texas swing about ex-wives and the states they lived in. At the edge of the tiny floor Tanner took her hand and moved into as much of a two-step as there was room for.

She had no trouble following him. He wasn't surprised. He'd always known she had the intelligence to maneuver her way through anything once she'd made up her mind.

What was she here for? "I hear you're doing pretty well," he said. "Hotshot reporter at KVCD."

She shook her head, smiling and looking a little abashed.

"Got your own cameraman . . ."

"No—it's more like he's got me. He's the technical pro. I'm working with him on this project only."

"On your way up?"

"I hope so."

"I hope so, too, then."

She drew in a breath that lifted her breasts under the gold sweater. Beneath his hand her back felt warm, straight, supple, with the strength of well-toned muscles. He wondered what it would feel like to hold her against him, to have the length of her body against his, his mouth pressed against the side of her neck, her hair brushing his face.

He'd never danced with her before. He'd kept his hands off her, and only thought about holding her.

"I'm sorry . . . about Buck," he said, wanting to get out what needed to be said between them.

"Thank you. So am I. Most of the time."

Most of the time? He frowned, assessing her answer. "And I'm sorry I couldn't make it to the funeral."

"I . . . know. You would have been there if you could."

"I hope you believe that." *She would have, if she'd read his letters.*

Julie didn't acknowledge the reference. She gave him a quick glance, then dismissed the personal implications with a huff of breath. "All the riders got together after the funeral and made the stock contractor get rid of that bull. I guess they figured better late than never."

Better late than never? The words echoed in Tanner's mind, bringing an image that was very different from the one she'd just spelled out, and he felt an answering stir in his body, unbidden but as predictable as Texas heat. Is that what this was? A late answer? All the times she'd come to bars looking for Buck, was she here tonight looking for him?

Not likely, he told himself, and even less likely for what you've got in mind. But the surge of purely masculine hope ignored common sense.

"You're in the top ten for Cowboy of the Year, I've heard," she said, smiling at him again. "You're doing pretty well."

"As long as my luck holds."

"Oh, it's not all luck. Is it?"

"You were on the circuit long enough to know how much is luck, Julie. You tell me."

And while you're at it, tell me what you're here for.

"Maybe I want to hear it from you," she said lightly.

Tanner spread his fingers on her back and increased the pressure of his hand, steering her around so that her face was illuminated by the colored lights from the jukebox.

"Why?" he said.

She hesitated a fraction of a second before she gave him another bright and easy smile. "You're the one to ask, aren't you? One of the top ten?"

"And you're after an interview, is that it?" he asked, an edge in his voice.

Her brown eyes sparked with something he didn't want to see. She didn't speak.

Anger shot through him, fueled by his own gullibility. He'd wanted to believe something that should have stayed in the category of fantasy, and the reality was a sharp reminder of how easily Julie Fielding could throw him. He should have realized it when he hit the dirt that afternoon. "That's what you're here for, Julie? You need a comment for your movie?"

She missed her first step, but recovered so quickly, only Tanner noticed it. It was enough to give him his answer though.

On the jukebox the record changed, and Jesse Wilson's rough voice came over the speakers in a slow, crooning ballad about mistakes and broken hearts. Tanner let his palm drop from Julie Fielding's back, then moved away from her and shoved his hands into his pockets. "I can't stop you from taking pictures of me in the dirt, lady," he said deliberately, "but I'm sure as hell not going to describe it for you."

On the jukebox Jesse Wilson sang, "I should have walked away before you smiled," and Tanner

Danielson cursed himself for not doing just that. Spine stiff, he started to turn away.

"Tanner . . ."

Her hand on his arm, and the plea in her voice, stopped him in midstep. "Tanner, that isn't what I came for. Not . . . not entirely."

He turned around and faced her gaze. Innocent as sin, and twice as dangerous.

"Buck was . . . a friend of yours. And I needed—"

"Buck's been dead a lot of years," he said, cutting her off. "This isn't about Buck."

"It's not that simple, Tanner. Things aren't that . . . uncomplicated. You can't expect everything to be black and white."

Her hand was still on his arm, heating his skin through the material of his shirt, sending messages all through the tensed muscles of his body. He glanced down at her fingers. "You want to dance or not?" he said harshly.

Her exhaled breath made a tiny sound. She caught her lip between her teeth, looked down at the floor, then moved her hand away from his arm. It trembled when she let go of him.

"Yes or no?" he asked.

She stared at him, silent, while she swallowed.

He moved toward her and reached for her hand. This time there was no two-step. Tanner spread his fingers on her back and drew her close enough to make it more than a dance.

Not sure why she'd let him take her answer as yes, Julie moved into the dance in slow motion, feeling as if the room around them had changed pace, to match the wave of slow heat that radiated between them. Her hand was wrapped in his, palm to palm, while he controlled the scant distance between them with a bronc rider's finesse. Sensations rippled through her at the warmth of his hands.

"I took one look at you, and I fell hard," the voice on the jukebox crooned again. The dim light in the bar shifted and moved over the planes of Tanner's face and the dark hair beneath the brim of his hat. As far as she could tell, his hair was the same color it had been thirteen years ago, when she hadn't let herself see it this close. Her gaze dropped to the collar of his shirt, then lower to the opened top button, where his shirt was pulled taut across his chest, delineating the almost square pectoral muscles, the hollow above his collarbone, and the powerful curve of his broad shoulders.

She had to tip her head back to look again at his face—the slightly crooked nose and narrow jaw, the old scar halfway between his chin and his left ear. His blue eyes were disconcerting as they assessed her slowly, thoroughly, and on his own terms.

"I always wondered if you knew how to dance, Jule," he said.

"I didn't when I was eighteen."

"Learned a lot since you were eighteen?"

A flicker of anger darkened her expression. "A lot of the *simple* things I already knew by then," she snapped back. "If all you're looking for is yes or no, it makes everything pretty easy, doesn't it?"

He studied her, then, with leisurely, half-insolent appraisal, let his gaze rove down to her mouth, her throat, the swell of her breasts, the curve of her hips outlined by the white chinos. "I guess it does at that," he said. His hand on her back pulled her against him, and he stepped into the embrace in an easy, almost casual move that brought her body into full contact with his, her breasts to his chest, her thighs along the length of his legs, her hips flat against the masculine juncture that more than hinted of blatant arousal.

It didn't matter that the close dancing was nothing more than most of the couples around them were engaged in, or that, according to the social mores of the Hoof and Horn, the embrace was socially permissible flirtation. Julie felt the impact of Tanner's body as if he'd just kicked shut a bedroom door, and her treacherous, suddenly explosive imagination provided all the details of what would take place there. A penetrating, subtle heat flowed through her, making her wonder what it would feel like to let this man's hands rove over her, caressing her, unsnapping and unbuttoning and drawing off her clothes, doing what his body implied he was doing in his mind.

She swallowed past the dryness in her throat and pressed a palm against his shoulder. She pushed ineffectually against him while her face, too close to his, tipped up toward him, and she felt panic showing in her eyes. "I . . . I don't . . ." She broke off, breathless, too flustered to finish, much too shaken by the slow fever that suffused her.

Tanner took in the flush of color that tinted her cheeks and felt his own answering desire to the warmth pressed against him. Julie Fielding didn't have the cynical, professional moves it took to be a barfly. She was smart, gutsy, and, he suspected, good at what she did. But for all her professional motives, she shimmered against him with an untapped sensuality that made him heat up in immediate, urgent response.

And it scared the hell out of her.

The quick, angry satisfaction he'd felt in coming

on to her drained away. A memory he'd been fighting all night glimmered, then coalesced, in his mind: a vulnerable, scared young woman, trying gallantly to do what couldn't be done— salvage her young marriage, save Buck from himself, deny her own needs.

He hadn't pushed her then. He couldn't do it now.

Slowly, reluctantly, Tanner reined in the savage need that ran through him like a spring-flooded river. His hand tightened on her back as his body stiffened in a final protest, then relaxed, muscle by muscle. He let his hand fall, let her step away from him, then shut his eyes while the realization washed over him that he still wanted her, just the way he had when he was twenty-two. Maybe more. And there wasn't anything simple about it.

He let out a long, shuddering breath. "Okay, then," he said, almost as if it were a decision. He opened his yes, met her gaze, and hooked his thumbs into his belt loops. "You want to talk? That's what you came for?"

He read surprise and confusion in her gaze, but the response she gave, whether or not she had to force herself into it, was a slight, single nod.

"Okay. We'll talk."

The brown eyes held his for a moment, then her gaze moved to the jukebox, the crowded dance floor, the fully occupied tables. "Is there . . . someplace that might be better for listening?"

"There's a couple of picnic tables down the bottom of the hill outside, beside the stream. That okay?"

She nodded.

"I'll get us a couple of beers."

"I don't . . ." The protest died as she watched him. "Okay. Fine."

He didn't ask again. He put his hand on Julie Fielding's shoulder, careful to touch her with just his fingertips, turned her around, and walked her toward the bar.

Two

The moment he let go of her shoulder to reach for his wallet, Julie took a step away from him, utterly unsettled by her own reaction to that last dance. Her body still tingled in all the places he'd been pressed against, and she could still feel that unexpected, intoxicating rush of being on the pinnacle of something precariously balanced between fantasy and fatal mistake.

She straightened her spine and forced herself to look at Tanner Danielson. Thirty-five years old, she reminded herself, not twenty-two. Top contender for Cowboy of the Year, not the brash, cool rider admired for his daring and his style. An interview subject for Nick's documentary, not a piece of her past.

The back of his pale gray shirt was creased in the middle, as if it had been taken out of a suitcase just before he put it on. Halfway down his back, under the material of the shirt, she could see the outline of white adhesive tape.

Taped ribs? The small detail jolted a recollection before she could stifle it.

"You can't ride that way."

She was standing beside the rails with Buck while Tanner climbed over, glancing over his shoulder at her impulsive comment, one that was out of line by rodeo standards. "I'll be all right, Julie," he'd answered, grinning, cutting off Buck's reprimand to a wife who was supposed to keep quiet around the riders. "But I sure appreciate the concern."

Disturbed by the ease with which the memory returned, Julie watched Tanner's hand stuff the billfold into the back pocket of his jeans. Before she looked away, he turned around and caught her staring in the general direction of his fly.

She flushed crimson, then jerked her gaze up where it belonged and met Tanner's. His expression was bland, too carefully blank for him to have missed her reaction.

"Here you go." He offered one of the beers.

Her gaze fell to the strong, dark hand wrapped around the tall bottle. An unexpected shiver touched her like cool air on heated skin. Take it, and this game's as good as lost, she thought suddenly, but she reached for the bottle.

"Thanks," she managed to say. It sounded forced, and she was aware of her heart pounding in her chest as Tanner stepped in front of her to lead the way through the crowd toward the open door.

The air outside was cool and moist, with a hint, even on this clear July evening, of the heavy rains that watered this mountainous Oregon ranch country—the first stop in Julie's six-week schedule of rodeos. Evening stars glimmered in the dusky sky. They made their way past a few bar patrons leaning against the stair rail, then crossed the parking lot side by side. She kept her elbows close to her waist so that she wouldn't touch him.

At the edge of the lot, where the wooded ground sloped down to a small clearing circled by trees, Tanner stepped in front of her and took her arm. The warmth of his hand was shocking in contrast to the cold, wet bottle she was holding and the cool, lush grass brushing her bare toes through her sandals.

The noise from the bar faded as they made their way toward the picnic tables. There was an unsettling sense of intimacy in the quiet, private grove of trees just next door to a crowded roadhouse. The rippling of the brook almost masked the tinny music from the jukebox, and a faint breeze stirred the leaves above them.

Tanner let go of her, walked around the picnic table toward the river, and stood facing it. Julie watched him in silence, assessing his motive for coming out here and giving a fleeting thought to her own. The attraction he held for her—maverick cowboy, ex-con, roughneck—was too strong to deny. He had the same dangerous charisma that had first drawn her to Buck, but with Tanner, even back then, an element of pure sensuality seemed to pulse beneath every innocent encounter.

"How come you never wear a hat?" he'd asked her once, long ago. When she'd muttered something about wearing it tomorrow, he'd watched her for a minute, then said, "No . . . don't." His hand had moved toward her hair. He'd stopped before he touched her, but she'd felt a shiver of reaction, the same one she'd experienced minutes earlier, when she'd danced with him.

She wrapped her hands around her beer, using

the cold bottle to keep herself grounded in the present.

Thirteen years. Thirteen years of wisdom. Thirteen years of experience. They should be enough to keep her from making a fool of herself, shouldn't they? She wasn't here for romance. She was after a preliminary interview, progress she could report to Nick when she got back. She had a job to do here: to get Tanner to talk. She couldn't afford to forget that.

She slipped her leather bag off her shoulder and dropped it on the table, then sat on the wooden bench, elbows in front of her on either side of the bag.

Tanner turned to study her. "You have a tape recorder in that bag?" he said suddenly.

She fell still for a moment, watching him warily. His face, under the brim of the Stetson, was defined by deepening night shadows and faint pink neon light from the sign of the neighboring bar. She couldn't read his expression.

"Yes," she said finally. She pulled the recorder out of the bag and set it on the table beside her, in Tanner's view. "Would it bother you if I turned it on?"

There was a moment's pause while Tanner drank from his beer, raised one booted foot to the bench opposite her, and rested his forearm across his knee. The grooves at the corners of his mouth creased, as if in response to some sort of private humor. "You think that's going to stop me from saying what you don't want to hear?"

"I'm not sure I know what you mean," she said carefully.

"You knew what I meant a few minutes ago," he

said. "When I lit your fire on that dance floor in there."

She drew in a sharp breath, feeling her cheeks flame under cover of the gathering darkness. "I don't remember you being quite so arrogant, Tanner."

He studied her a moment. "Go ahead and turn it on. If I say anything that isn't suitable for TV, you can just bleep it out. And pretend you never heard it."

She switched on the machine, ignoring the fact that her hand wasn't quite steady. "I don't remember you being so . . . blunt either."

"When you've done time, honey, you come out either more honest or more of a liar," he said, a dry note in his voice. "It's been a long time since I bothered to tell any lies."

"You didn't bother to tell any lies that I recall before you did time, anyway," she said, keeping her voice cool beneath the disturbing emotional backwash he seemed able to stir even when he wasn't holding her close on a dance floor. "You just didn't say much of anything about it—the case, the sentence, why you were going to prison."

"You could have asked Buck."

She blinked, taken aback by the unexpected comment, wondering what he meant by it. "I did," she said after a moment. "He knew you had some trouble with the border patrol. Over an illegal immigrant. A girl."

Tanner's eyes reflected a flicker of something that might have been challenge, or the kind of grim amusement that passed for cowboy tolerance. She couldn't puzzle it out. He didn't offer an explanation.

"Nobody expected you to go to jail for it," Julie

said into the lengthening silence. "A first offense."

"Maybe people should have. Her daddy worked with the minister of cultural affairs in Mexico City. He had a lot of friends in the Texas legal system."

The tape spun while she waited for him to fill in the rest. When he didn't respond, she softly supplied, "And she was underage."

Anger flashed in his face, then it was gone. He tipped his head back and let out a single huff of dry laughter. "You're good at this job, aren't you?"

Julie sighed and leaned a little farther away from the tape recorder. Not good enough, she thought.

"I always knew you had the stuff to make it, no matter what happened between you and Buck."

"You knew more than I did, then," she said dryly.

"I knew more than you were willing to admit, maybe." He rested his beer against his thigh, watching her. He was clearly leading her to ask him what he meant, but the automatic reporter's question didn't come to her lips. He was right, she realized, surprised at herself. She *had* been hoping to keep him from talking about what she didn't want to hear. Above the murmur of the brook the hiss of the tape recorder was just audible. "Things change as you get older," she said evenly.

"Some things do."

"Things have changed a little in the rodeo arena, haven't they?" she said quickly. "They've gotten even better for you. You've been winning a lot of rodeos. What's it like?"

He shrugged. "You know what it's like. You were there. When you're winning, there's nothing like going on down the road. All the broken bones and hard traveling and living on fast food and rodeo dirt—that doesn't seem to mean much when you're getting all the spoils of the game."

"The spoils?"

He took a swallow of beer. "Money. Glory. The lady of your choice. Provided she sees it that way." He rested the bottle against his raised thigh. "Provided she's not married to some other cowboy."

She held herself still against the shower of sensation that touched all her nerve endings and brought back emotions she shouldn't have been feeling after thirteen years.

Tanner pushed himself away from the bench, ambled around the table, and sat, straddled, beside her, elbow propped beside the tape recorder, bottle resting on his knee as he leaned toward her.

She was a reporter, she reminded herself. A professional businesswoman. A mother. She shouldn't be vulnerable to this kind of innuendo. "There's not much of a trick to finding girls at a rodeo," she said tartly, as much to remind herself of it as to keep Tanner at a distance.

His gaze narrowed. "Or in a bar on a Saturday night, I guess."

Her answer didn't get any further than a half-audible sound in the back of her throat.

"When I saw you on that barstool, and you got up and walked straight across the room, I had the feeling maybe things had changed some. That maybe you didn't have as much to hide these days, Jule."

The breeze died, as if the nickname she hadn't used since she was eighteen had stopped it. "What is it you think I'm hiding?" she said in defense against the volatile emotions that wanted to run riot inside her.

"You used to work pretty hard at pretending it was my fault when Buck got drunk, or didn't come home, or gambled away all his money," he said. "Part of it was makin' excuses for Buck. I know that. But part of it was to keep you from thinking about us. And you damn well knew you wanted to think about us."

"You think you *damn well knew* what I wanted?" she said, her voice sharp, giving in to anger because she didn't want to give in to the dangerous, uncontrollable emotions that ran just below the surface of her mind. "And what was that? To be part of the spoils of battle? Third on the list behind money and glory—until the luck runs out, and there isn't enough money and glory left to pay for the motel where you've been living?"

"Is that the way Buck left you? No money, no one to help?"

She didn't answer him, regretting her unprofessional outburst.

"What about Buck's friends?"

She raised her chin, looking out across the river, then shook her head once. "They didn't know."

Tanner's breath whooshed out. "You could've asked someone for help. "

"Who?" She looked at him. "You? You were in prison, Tanner. Remember?"

His fist tightened, along with a muscle in his jaw, and he swore under his breath. "Buck didn't have any money saved? Any plans for the future?"

She gave him a humorless smile. "I can't think of any future Buck wanted badly enough to save for."

"What every cowboy wants. A few hundred acres of grazing land, enough cattle to make a good herd, some bucking stock with the right bloodlines for rodeo broncs. A ranch. A family. Kids."

"Kids? When did Buck ever want kids?" Her fingers tightened unconsciously around the bottle as Skye's image flashed into her mind: turned-up nose and green eyes, just like her father's. But Buck was a man who hadn't really wanted kids. Who hadn't really wanted a wife, for that matter.

Tanner grabbed her beer bottle out of her suddenly nerveless fingers, and she glanced down at it, surprised.

"You don't want to spill that," he said, watching her.

"No. I . . ." She let out a quick, jerky breath, and her gaze flicked to his face.

In the quaking leaves of the trees the breeze whispered again. Julie glanced away from him, suddenly conscious of the spinning tape. "There wasn't much you could do, anyway. I was okay. I got a waitressing job in a coffee shop and . . . went on from there."

"A waitressing job?" he said tightly.

"It turned out all right," she said, her chin lifted. "I *did* go on from there. I have a career, a little security . . . everything I need."

"Do you?"

She stared at him, her eyes wide in the darkness. "What do you mean?"

"You were married when I knew you before," he said with that blunt honesty she found so disconcerting. "You married now?"

"I . . . I don't . . ."

"Anyone in your life you want to tell me about?"

"I—" She broke off, her heart pounding as Skye's image rose in her mind, and her panicked gaze searched his face for signs that he'd somehow found out about her daughter. He was frowning at her, his eyes narrowed, and she let her glance slip away from his, realizing the chance reference hadn't meant he knew about Skye. But her throat had gone dry, and she knew she didn't want him to find out.

She couldn't have said why. Only that it had something to do with the tarnish on her young marriage, with the pounding anger she'd felt at Buck for getting on that bull and leaving her alone with an unborn child to provide for, with the bitter knowledge that even her unconsciously wanted "careless" pregnancy wasn't going to save her from her own bad choices.

She hadn't told anyone on the rodeo circuit about her pregnancy. She'd kept her desperate secret to herself, terrified that letting it out would have sucked her and her baby back into that trap of dust and beer and the endless gamble of going on down the road.

She felt Tanner's gaze on the side of her face and made herself glance back at him fleetingly. "I'm . . . committed to myself and my career," she said breathlessly, her pulse drumming.

There was a charged silence. She moved her hand toward the tape recorder, nervously tracing the shape of the machine. "I'm committed to this project," she repeated. "That's what I'm here for. I want to make the best documentary on rodeo ever filmed, and with Nick's technical experience, we can—"

Tanner leaned forward, brushing her shoulder, and pushed the Stop button on the tape recorder.

She pulled her fingers back as if she'd got an electric shock.

"I don't have much interest in your cameraman's experience, lady," he said brusquely. "I don't particularly want to be a TV star, no matter how good the shot is when I hit the dust."

She flushed. "I . . . told you, we wouldn't use that shot if you object to it."

"You'll use whatever you have to if you really care about making your documentary," he growled. "Just like I'll use whatever I can to stay on a bronc for eight seconds. But that doesn't have a damn thing to do with why we're out here."

"I thought you agreed to . . . talk. . . ."

"Talk goes both ways, Jule. You want to talk about your documentary?" He moved his hand a few inches higher, so that the back of his knuckles just grazed her hair. "Give me a reason to care about it."

"I . . . you might take the title this year, Tanner. You have a real chance at it, and you . . ." Her eyes widened, and the words trailed off as she swallowed.

"I told you, Jule. I don't want to be a movie star."

She stared at him, her gaze locked with his for a fraught moment. Then, without a word, Tanner swept the two beer bottles into one fist, reached for her arm, and pulled her to her feet. He let go of her, picked up the tape machine and her bag, and thrust them into her hands.

Disoriented, she just managed to grab them before they dropped to the ground.

"I'll walk you back to your car."

She murmured startled, automatic thanks, and Tanner took her arm to help her up the hill. He dropped it at the edge of the parking lot, still silent.

"Tanner—" she started.

He kept his face impassive.

"Whatever I said to offend you, I didn't mean it that way."

He stopped for a moment and looked at her. "I'm not offended," he said, but his mouth was tight.

Julie clutched her bag close to her body as they crossed the parking lot. She gave him a nervous smile before she got into her car, then let out a quick, resigned breath and reached for the ignition, keys in her hand.

Tanner watched her, his jaw clenched against the emotions churning in his gut. Apparently she didn't intend to say good-bye. Just as she hadn't answered his letters.

Probably just as well, Tanner told himself. But before she could start the car, he leaned down and rested his forearms on the top of the window and waited for her gaze to meet his.

He lifted his hand to tip his hat back on his head. "I don't have any place interfering with the way you feel about Buck," he said gruffly. "You were married to him. He was a friend of mine."

"I . . . know that, and—"

"But anything that happens here and now is between you and me," he said, ignoring her interruption. "You got that?"

"I . . ." She didn't have an answer, and Tanner didn't wait for it. He straightened, stepped back from her door, and stood in the parking lot, hands in his pockets, watching while she started the car and pulled away from him.

He was still watching when he saw her glance into the rearview mirror to see if he was still there.

Three

The vision of Tanner Danielson watching her was still in her mind when Julie let herself in her motel room, and dropped her bag on the bed. It tipped to one side and gaped open, unbalanced by the tape recorder she'd hastily stuffed inside. Julie stared at the machine while she pressed two fingers against her lips.

The tape, from Nick's point of view, would be all but useless. Tanner hadn't given her more than a paragraph of information.

From *her* point of view it was worse than useless. It was evidence of how badly she'd blown it. How irrationally vulnerable she'd been to Tanner Danielson, in a cowboy bar in Roseburg, the night after a rodeo.

And that moment when he'd touched her hair, and she'd thought he was going to kiss her . . .

She pressed a palm against the side of her neck, and massaged her jaw as she tipped her head back and let her eyes slide shut. The truth was, she would have let him, because close up, Tanner

Danielson held sway over her senses in a way that mesmerized her. He always had.

Dear Julie . . .

I wish I knew why some things happen the way they do. . . . If thinking about you could unlock this cell and put me in Wyoming, I would have been there already. . . .

She opened her eyes, staring at the wall across the room, seeing instead a letter written from a Texas jail cell thirteen years ago that had been devastating to her fragile emotional balance. She hadn't answered it. She hadn't answered the one after it, either, or the one after that. She'd been afraid, in her worry and her uncertainty and her desperate loneliness, of what she would say. And she'd had just enough self-protective instinct to know she couldn't risk saying anything.

It had taken her thirteen years to get over that fear. And she *was* over it. Wasn't she?

She realized she was staring again at the tape recorder, hearing in her mind the sound of Tanner's husky, intimate words.

Anyone in your life you want to tell me about?

With decisive steps she paced to the nightstand, reached for the phone, and dialed.

Skye picked up on the second ring. "Hello?" The bright, impatient voice brought, as always, a lift of joy and an ache of longing.

"Hi, honey," Julie said.

"Mom!" The phone line crackled as Skye banged the receiver on something, calling, "It's Mom," over her shoulder. "Rosa didn't think you'd call till later," Skye said into the phone.

"I wanted to hear your voice, honey. What are you doing now?"

Skye laughed. "Talking to you," she said, using

the standard reply to the old family joke. "Kids have been calling me all night. Rosa says I spend too much time on the phone."

Rosa, their grandmotherly next-door neighbor, had been Skye's baby-sitter since she was four. "Rosa's probably right."

"But what am I supposed to do, Mom? All these kids *call* me!"

The tone of feigned exasperation at her popularity brought a smile to Julie's face. Skye, at thirteen, was outgoing, sociable, and precocious. "What do you talk about during all these phone calls?" she asked.

"Well, you know . . ." Julie could hear the shrug. "I had to tell everyone about you being at the rodeo, Mom. They all thought it was really mint. Did you get to meet any cowboys yet?"

"A couple," Julie said.

"Radical! Who?"

"I'm not here to meet cowboys, Skye," she said, hearing the overly prim note in her own voice. "I'm here to do a job."

There was a pause, then Skye huffed into the phone, sounding very adult, "Well, I know *that*, Mom. When will you be home?"

"Three weeks. Seattle's not too far from the rodeo circuit. I'll be able to get a few days off then."

"Okay." Another pause. "Can we go shopping then? I really need some new clothes, Mom. I don't have anything to wear in case I go—in case I have to go anywhere, you know?"

"Sure." Julie smiled. "We'll go shopping when I get back. Will that be soon enough?"

"Well . . . I guess so."

"Put Rosa on, okay? Love you, honey."

"Me too," her daughter echoed.

Rosa's lilting, grandmotherly voice replaced Skye's. Julie listened to the day's events, exchanged mundane good-byes, and put the phone back, reassured, as always, by the sound of Skye's voice and Rosa's familiar brand of no-nonsense compassion.

Skye would be fine, she told herself, for the three weeks her mother was away. She had what she needed. What they both needed: love, security, enough money to maintain a comfortable way of life and provide for Skye's education, a stable, reliable relationship . . .

Nothing was going to disrupt that. Julie took a deep breath, let it out, and felt her mouth tip upward in a wan smile. She'd given Skye all that. She'd given herself that. From the desperation she'd felt after Buck's death, she'd built a stable, secure life to raise her daughter.

"Okay," she said aloud. "So tonight wasn't much in the way of an interview. It was the first time I've seen him. I didn't know what to expect."

It took her a moment to realize she was staring at the tape recorder as if it could talk back. "All right! I was . . . a little besotted," she told the accusing machine. "He's got plenty of charisma, and he's as photogenic as the whole damn state of Montana, and he asked too many questions." She let out a long breath, her gaze focused somewhere above the motel-room bed. "At least I wasn't fool enough to answer them. And it won't happen again. Next time I'll be the one collecting answers."

"Way to go, cowboy," one of the stock handlers called out.

From the top of the rails Tanner grinned, then

leaned over and hefted his saddle from the bronc that had just given him an eighty-one-point ride. "I got a lucky draw," he commented.

"This is the town to get lucky in," the man answered back.

Holding the saddle, Tanner glanced across the stock pens toward the press corral. The glint of blond was right where he expected it to be, next to the big cameraman. Something pulled up tight in his gut—the same thing, he decided wryly, that had destroyed his concentration at the Roseburg rodeo. This time, he'd made a point of not looking at her until the buzzer sounded and the pickup man had given him a chance to get off the bronc right-side-up. Tanner hitched his saddle against his hip and jumped down to the sawdust-covered floor.

This time he'd won. Points, prize money, and that satisfying, unmistakable flash of something in Julie Fielding's brown eyes—relief, release of anxiety . . . admiration. There wasn't any mistake about that look. He could still feel it.

Out of sight at floor level behind the stock pens, he glanced again toward the press corral, realizing that Julie wasn't likely to admit her reaction. Not if her behavior outside the Hoof and Horn was any indication. He'd appreciated standing in that parking lot watching her drive away about as much as he appreciated a kick from a bull.

He ought to take her lead, let it go, end it now before it started. Hell, he should've let it go the first time he met her, before he'd put himself on a surprise track to the slammer.

And what did he know about her now? She worked for a Seattle TV station, but she was taking time out to work with a hotshot independent cameraman who seemed to know the ropes.

His mouth quirked sourly. And she was committed to her own career.

But that look in her eyes ten minutes ago wasn't professional interest.

And Tanner's gut, along with the other parts of his anatomy, told him he wasn't going to drop it.

The lights in the arena dimmed when half the crowd had filtered out of the Reno Events Center. Julie snapped the video case closed and listened to Nick's muttered curse.

"Why can't they leave the damn lights on long enough for the press crew to finish packing up?" he grumbled, squinting over his shoulder at the announcer's booth.

Julie grinned. "It's rodeo, Nick. They're not supposed to like the press."

"No? And it's not bad enough coating all the lenses with dust?"

"There was some good footage tonight, though."

He was silent for a moment, and she glanced back at him.

"Nothing like Danielson's ride in Roseburg," he commented when he caught her eye.

Julie looked away, feeling heat in her face that she told herself probably wasn't visible in the dimmed light. "I was wondering when you'd bring up that subject."

"You get anywhere with him the other night?" the cameraman inquired.

She set the video case in the sawdust beside Nick's camera and reached for a tripod. *The real question was how far Tanner had got with her.*

"As it turns out, no," she said. "He wasn't interested in being interviewed."

"No tape?"

"I got tape," Julie said tightly. "But there isn't much of anything on it."

Nick watched her fold the tripod, making no move to help, then shrugged. "Well, better luck next time."

"I hope so," she said shortly. "But we'd better face the fact that he might never cooperate enough, Nick."

"Sure he will," the cameraman muttered blithely.

"*I'm* not that sure," she stated. "He's not interested in talking to reporters."

The subdued buzz of the departing crowd undulated in the background, punctuated by the occasional lowing of a dissatisfied calf and the shouts of stock handlers. Julie snapped the tripod legs closed, and finally met Nick's interested gaze.

"Funny," he drawled, ignoring the equipment, "he talked to me."

She stopped winding a cord, feeling as if she'd been knocked down. Tanner had talked to Nick?

"When?" she asked.

"This afternoon," Nick said offhandedly. "After we set up, when you were headed for the announcer's booth."

She felt a surge of irritation she tried to suppress. She didn't succeed. Nick was enjoying showing off. "You looked him up this afternoon?"

Nick shook his head. "He found me. I got the feeling he was interested in finding out if I had a . . . claim, so to speak."

"A claim?"

Nick grinned at her, cat-smug, but with an assessing glint in his eye, watching her reaction.

Her jaw tightened. "That must have been a friendly little discussion."

"I told him I didn't," said Nick, unruffled.

Julie dropped the cord on top of the tripod. "What makes you think you had any right to tell him anything? What makes you think discussing me behind my back is anything you can stand here and justify to my face?"

Nick's eyebrows rose. "Did I touch a nerve here?"

"I don't like being played like a hostile interview, Nick."

"So come clean with me, and I won't have to do it," he snapped back.

"Come clean about what?"

He aimed a forefinger at her. "About your emotional involvement in this project. That's why you're here, isn't it?"

"I'm here to make a documentary," she flared at him. "And my involvement in it is professional, commercial, objective, and—and—"

"And what? Detached?"

She stared at him.

He took a step toward her and picked up the cord she'd dropped. "Let me tell you something, kiddo. No documentary ever made is worth a damn unless the filmmaker is emotionally involved in it, one way or another."

She snatched up the tripod and a light stand. "I'm bringing these out to the van, then I've got some errands to do. I'll take a cab."

"I'll tell you something else," Nick went on, as if she hadn't spoke. "Neither is a life."

Fuming, Julie strode outside, put the two pieces

of equipment in the van, and hitched her bag over her shoulder.

There wasn't a cab in sight.

Five minutes later, wondering when cabs had been banned in Reno, she walked back into the Events Center to avoid meeting Nick when he came out with the rest of the equipment. She fought her way through the crowd in the lobby and stepped into the relative quiet of the area behind the chutes.

The smell of sawdust and manure drifted around her, somehow more redolent in the dim backstage light than in the spotlights over the press corral. A few stock handlers trotted by her, carrying shovels or grain buckets, bent on finishing their jobs and heading out for a beer. Most of the cowboys had already left, no doubt with the same intention. Julie paused just inside the doors, beset by the ambience and a new set of memories. She hadn't been behind the stock pens in thirteen years. The place brought recollections, vivid, unexpected . . . and more emotionally involving than she wanted to admit.

She frowned, angry again at Nick's pronouncements. She *knew* what rodeo life was like. She wanted to film it, not live it again. She wanted to face up to her mistakes and put them in perspective, not make them all over again.

She gritted her teeth, mentally denying that Nick had hit any raw nerve. Tanner was part of her past, one of the few mistakes she *hadn't* made. She wasn't about to make it now.

One of the stockmen walked by her, grinned at someone over her shoulder, and called, "Hey, cowboy, good one this afternoon."

She glanced around, then shut her eyes, cursing

the bad luck that seemed to be dogging her. When she opened them, her luck hadn't changed.

"Tanner," she said.

He touched his hat. "Julie."

He was dressed to ride, in jeans, boots, and blue chamois shirt, with a pair of fringed chaps belted around his hips and tied at the knee. A coil of rope was around his wrist.

He pushed his hat back on his forehead. "What're you doing here?"

She let out a breath. She'd done it again. One look at him, and she'd let herself be put on the wrong end of a question. "I could ask you the same thing," she said. "I didn't think you were on the roster tonight."

"I wasn't." The blue eyes studied her a moment. "One of the ropers asked me to ride with him, but his regular hazer showed up before the event, so I was off the hook."

"Oh." She nodded, glancing at him again before she looked down. Buck would never have ridden hazer. He'd kept himself apart from the ropers, who traveled with horses and couldn't keep the same grueling circuit the roughstock riders did.

"Congratulations on your ride this afternoon," she said, a little too quickly. "That was quite a score."

"Yeah, well, you know how it goes. Half of it belongs to the horse."

She did know. She'd listened to enough complaints about a bad draw. She pulled her hands out of the pockets of her jumper and folded them across her rib cage in a protective gesture. "Even with a hard-bucking horse, though, you have to stay on, Tanner."

One corner of his mouth kicked up in a half-grin, but he wouldn't admit the truth of her statement. Cowboy modesty didn't allow acknowledgment of compliments.

She dropped her eyes again, and her gaze flicked over Tanner's rodeo garb. The chaps emphasized his narrow hips and lazy stance. His working-man's shirt, undecorated and threadbare at the elbows, wasn't up to rodeo standards, but he didn't need any decoration beyond strength and balance, grace in the arena, and blue eyes that were watching her with the same kind of intensity they'd held the night before.

I got the feeling he was interested in finding out if I had a claim, Nick had said. She felt herself responding to that hot blue gaze at the same time that a trickle of anger flared again in her mind. She didn't want to feel either. Not with Tanner Danielson's eyes on her.

A calf lowed in one of the pens nearby, and she jumped as if Tanner had touched her, then colored at the betrayal of tension.

Tanner's eyes stayed on her face. There was a long moment filled with the sound of a distant gate clanking open, the slosh of water in a trough, the murmur of men's voices—sounds familiar to both of them, or to anyone who'd spent time around rodeos.

That familiarity served as a stark contrast to Julie's nervousness as Tanner took in the signs of it. She stood perfectly still, but beneath the cool intelligence in her face he could see the ebb and flow of emotion that heated his own fire of response. She was wearing a loose white cotton dress that skimmed her body, hinting at the curves beneath it, the way her eyes hinted at passion beneath the reserve. He swallowed a sound in the back of his throat.

"Have you been followin' rodeo, all these years?" he asked.

She gave a shrug. "I've followed it on television. I guess . . . I guess it gets into your blood, or something."

There was a glint in his eyes. "I saw you, behind the rails, when I finished my ride. You still know how to watch, Jule."

"Yes, well," she said defensively, "that's my job."

"Right. Your job." One corner of his mouth turned up. "That what you're doing back here now?"

"You might say that." She indicated the pens with a small, self-conscious gesture, then pressed her hand against the side of her neck. "I was . . . absorbing atmosphere. Remembering what it was like."

"Where's your cameraman?"

She gave him a sharp look that made him wonder if she did have something going with Nick. The cameraman had denied it, Tanner reminded himself, and he'd thought at the time Nick was truthful. Blind, maybe, but truthful.

She shrugged. "He's packing up."

"So he's packing up, and you're taking in atmosphere."

"I thought we might use some shots back here. Rodeo behind the scenes. The stock contractors, the animals . . ."

"Yeah," Tanner said with a touch of irony. "Get it all on tape."

"What's wrong with that?"

"Nothing in particular. It's just not much of a substitute for the real thing."

"It's a job, all right?" She flung out one hand in an irritated gesture. "It's what I do for a living. I don't have to be emotionally involved in the stock pens to make a documentary on rodeo."

He wondered what had set her off. She fell still after the outburst, but he could see the beat of a pulse at her throat. *Would you be emotionally involved, honey, if I moved in close enough to feel the way your blood races under that smooth silk skin?* The thought made his own blood race, hot, fast, and definitely involved.

"Sorry," she muttered, trying to cover up the lapse in cool distance. "It's been a long day."

Tanner let the coil of rope slip down to his palm, closed his fingers around it, testing its weight, then looked up at her again. "Yeah. I know about long days. There aren't any other kind in rodeo."

"No, I guess there aren't."

He hooked the rope around his wrist again. "You always held up pretty well, though, as I remember. You still do all the driving, or does the civilized grizzly do his share?"

A reluctant smile chipped away at some of her defenses. "Nick likes to drive. That's one point in his favor."

"You never liked it. But you drove anyway," he said softly. "That's a point in yours."

"Somebody had to."

"That beat-up Chevy wagon of yours sounded like a tank in a minefield. Did it run as bad as it sounded?"

"Yes, I'm afraid it did," she said.

He shouldn't have brought it up, but the memory had sprung up in his mind like brazen prairie weeds after a rain. Tanner had found her asleep in that car one morning after she'd driven all night so

Buck could make the next day's rodeo. He'd brought her a cardboard cup of coffee and woke her up with a mumbled apology he hadn't meant. He'd been driving all night, too, and fatigue had made him reckless. She'd blinked at him, still half-asleep, smudges under her eyes, and he'd leaned in the window for a crazy moment and almost kissed her. She hadn't moved, hadn't backed away, and there had been something soft about her mouth.

He'd left the coffee on the dashboard, turned away, and walked back to the chutes to his ride without another word, without mention of the fact that he wasn't the one who should have been checking on her. He half wished he'd run into Buck so he could pick a fight.

"Cup of coffee, Jule?" he said now.

She met his eyes, her own expression wary, and he wondered if she was remembering the same incident.

"Come on. We can get something to eat. Unwind a little. Take some time off."

"I don't want . . . time off, Tanner. I'm here to do a job. I don't need to unwind. I need to get the job done." Yet she made no move to go anywhere.

He took a step closer, reached out and hung the rope on a folding gate, then hooked his thumb into the top of his chaps. "Yeah. Your job. I used to see you once in a while on television," he said softly, as if they'd never clashed over the subject of her job, "when you were a correspondent in wherever the hell you were reporting from."

She glanced up to meet his gaze, taken off guard, wishing she knew how to stem the wash of emotions he seemed capable of unleasing whenever he started to talk.

"It was kind of strange, seeing you there on that screen. I always wondered where you went when you were done, who you met, what you were doing with your life when you weren't working."

"I . . . didn't know you'd ever seen me. I wasn't a reporter that long."

He nodded, silent, waiting for her to fill in the answers to the not-quite-asked questions.

But the answers didn't come to her lips. Skye—the reason for her dedication to her job, the focus of her personal life—was the detail she should tell him now, but the constraints she'd felt outside the bar in Roseburg were still with her. And she didn't want to encourage the intimacy that had slipped around them like mist, making the semipublic stockyard seem private, close, fraught with shared personal history.

"Tanner, I don't . . ." Not knowing what she wanted to say, she let her words trail off with an involuntary, breathy catch in her voice.

"You don't," he repeated softly, dismissing the words. He touched her hair, brushed it back from her shoulder, than traced the outline of her jaw with one fingertip, the gesture light, easy, almost casual.

Julie's stomach fluttered. She felt a tightness in her chest, a heaviness in the lower part of her body that sapped her will to step away from him.

"Tanner, my life is very different now. I'm involved with . . ."

Something flickered in his eyes and his finger stilled. "Involved with . . . ?" he said, waiting for her to answer.

"With my work, and . . . and my life in Seattle . . . the station . . ."

"Yeah, you said. Videotape."

"Yes. Videotape."

His fingers cupped the back of her neck, caressing. "Maybe you should try the real thing, Jule," he murmured.

She tried to move away from him, but with a slight pressure, he brought her toward him. "I've tried the real thing, Tanner. I don't want to try it again."

"Leave Buck out of this," he said, his voice a husky warning. "He doesn't belong here."

"Neither do I."

His fingers massaged the back of her neck. "You're probably right. But don't try to tell me you never wondered what it would be like. Never imagined what might happen . . ."

She let her eyes slide shut, as helpless to move away as if he held her captive. He smelled of saddle soap, leather, and some vague scent of evergreen forest. When she opened her eyes, his face was a little closer. He'd shaved recently. After his ride, it must have been. He'd always shaved before he went out for the evening when she'd known him. It was an elusive point of cowboy chivalry she'd once found compellingly sexy.

She still did, she realized, admitting it as if she were sinking into a deep, sensual mist that had no bottom and no limits.

Yes, she'd wondered. Every time she'd reread his letters. Every time she'd seen a rodeo on TV. She'd tried not to. She'd told herself it was just compulsive curiosity, leftover adolescent fantasy, the kind of urge she'd never give in to. But she'd wondered, and since she'd danced with him, the urge to discover what it would be like had been so strong, it had turned her throat dry and made her heart beat wildly everywhere she could feel a pulse.

His hands circled her shoulders, brushed down over her arms, then caught her wrists, and put her fingers on his waist.

The warm, dim bustle of the stock pens faded into obscurity as his head tipped down to hers, and his hat brim shadowed the lights hanging high overhead.

"Tanner . . . don't."

"I've spent some time thinking about where you might belong, Julie," he said gruffly.

He threaded his hands into her hair again, lowered his head the remaining distance between them, and touched her mouth with his, holding her lightly while he brushed his lips across hers in an unhurried caress.

Her eyes closed, and the lightest of shivers ran down her spine. Tanner's hand followed it, brushing along her neck, then sliding down her back, urging her a little closer to him.

Her resistance melted in the warmth of Tanner's mouth on hers, and she leaned toward him and flattened her palms against his sides.

He wrapped her in his arms, fitting their bodies together so that all the sensitive places were pressed close. She felt the warm, wet tip of his tongue slide along her lips, urging them open, stroking and persuading and driving away any faint voice of warning that still whispered in the back of her mind.

Her lips parted, and the slow, hot glide of his tongue sought the intimacy of her mouth. She gave it, meeting his tongue with her own, tilting her head when the gentle pressure of his palm demanded it, fitting their mouths together for a searching, wholly consuming kiss that made the world disappear and turned her body to sweet liquid fire.

For a moment after Tanner's mouth lifted from hers, she was aware only of the sudden feeling of deprivation, then a low, surprised whistle from the direction of the stock pens brought the distinct and unwelcome realization of where they were.

"Ride 'em cowboy," the stockman muttered, grinning at them and giving a thumbs-up before he rounded the corner of the pen.

A flood of heat washed over Julie with the acknowledgment of how far she'd let the kiss go, and what she'd just done.

Tanner's eyes were a deep, intense blue, watching her seriously. He hadn't so much as glanced at the man whose comment had brought Julie back to earth.

"Again, Jule," he said softly.

He urged her toward him again, but some measure of her common sense had returned. She pushed his arms away and stepped back from him. "No."

He grasped her shoulders for a moment, then, as if it had finally occurred to him they weren't in a private place, he glanced around and let her go. His eyes darkened for a moment, then he let out a breath, smiled with one corner of his mouth, and said, "I guess we could've picked a better place."

"No, that's . . . that's not the issue."

He reached toward her cheek, and she tipped her head away. "I'm not interested in a quick roadside affair, Tanner."

"Maybe that's not what I'm interested in either," he said. "You ever think to ask?" The soft growl sent goose bumps shivering up her spine.

"But you can't offer anything else!" She gestured

with her hands as though she would have pushed his arms away again. "That's just the point, Tanner! You *live* on the road. And I know what that's like." She wrapped her arms around herself, hugging her elbows close to her body in a protective gesture. "I know firsthand what that's like."

She turned on her heel and walked toward the door.

"Julie—"

She didn't answer as she pushed through the door. Tanner took a couple of steps after her, then stopped in the doorway. It wouldn't do any good to follow, he told himself. He couldn't argue with her.

He kicked the door in frustration and propped it open with the heel of his boot then watched as Julie hurried through the lobby away from him, breaking into a run every third or fourth step. He was aware that it took a certain kind of fool to stand and let a woman walk away. Again.

But then, Julie Fielding wasn't walking. Her agitation was evident in every movement, in every line of her body.

She'd felt that kiss as much as he had. *She* couldn't argue with that.

And what the hell did words have to do with it, anyway?

Four

The dirt on the camera cases was thick enough to write the station numbers in when Nick gave up grumbling about it. They'd covered three rodeos and five hundred miles in two days. The pace was exhausting, but it was one they'd have to keep up if they intended to document the six weeks' progress for the top half-dozen cowboys. It was no more grueling than the pace of the cowboys themselves. Prize money was accumulated ride by ride, and the top contenders scheduled as many rodeos as possible in the circuit they followed.

They filmed Tanner only twice. Julie didn't see him at all outside the arena, but whether working or snatching a hamburger and a soda between shoots, she couldn't seem to go any place without hearing his name. She should have expected it, she told herself. They were on the rodeo circuit, but her last encounter with Tanner had been disturbing enough to make her want to forget it, and every mention of his name frayed her nerves.

By Thursday morning Nick had made her preoccupation a standard jibe, and over breakfast, when he tipped her clipboard toward him to read her roster notes and found it blank, he gave her a smirk and muttered, "Which rodeos we headed for, kiddo?"

"The finals in Reno day after tomorrow," Julie snapped back at him. "Then we drive to Colorado and start shooting the Greeley Stampede on Tuesday. Until tomorrow night we stay in Lehi. Hotchkins is fifth on the roster, on Piece O'Cake. It should be a good ride if he stays on."

Nick grinned at her, signaled the coffee-shop waitress for a refill on his cup, and gave another glance to her clipboard. "Should be a good ride, huh?"

"That's right. If you get decent footage, Nick," she told him, matching his tone, "it can go to KBZF in Salt Lake City."

"The local station?"

She nodded. "They're interested in Hotchkins because he's a local. I've got him scheduled for an interview tomorrow morning. We'll have to get up early."

Nick's eyebrows rose. "Been busy, have you?"

The waitress, in a cowboy hat that said I LOVE RODEO COWBOYS on the hatband, appeared at their booth, poured their coffee, then grinned cheerfully. "That be all, folks?"

"That's it," Nick told her. She scribbled their check and left it on the table. Nick watched her swish toward the next table, withholding comment, then picked up his mug and sipped, studying Julie over the rim, withholding comment on her as well.

"It's good advance publicity for the documentary," Julie said coolly. "And a little free-lance money."

"Not to mention evidence of your abilities as future program director, eh?"

Julie raised her chin. "Yes. I want that job."

He studied her a moment, then said unexpectedly, "You're better at this one. You'll be wasted in the office."

"At least I'll be home every night."

"Yep," Nick said wryly. "And Skye will still act like a teenager, kiddo. They all do."

"I intend to be there when it happens," she said, a little sharply, then made a face and shrugged an apology for the snappish tone. "The phone's been busy three of the last five times I've tried to get through. Rosa says Skye's been calling some sixteen-year-old boy I've never heard about. Rosa says the only thing she knows about him is he has his own car and he—"

"What?" Nick asked when Julie broke off and glanced down at the table, fingers pressed to the bridge of her nose.

Julie's shoulders lifted and fell resignedly. "He wears a cowboy hat."

Nick made a philosophical hum in the back of his throat. "Is he calling her back?"

"How do I know?" Julie flared. "I'm not even there."

"Rosa will keep a lid on it. You don't have to worry."

"Easy for you to say. Your two are grown up. And they had two parents to begin with."

"They all have two parents to begin with, kiddo." He watched her, his eyes narrowed, his shrewd mind obviously busy for speculation. "You ever talk to Skye about her father?"

"What do you mean?" She drew herself up a little straighter in the chair and pulled her clipboard toward her in a protective gesture. "She never even saw her father."

"So? That means she never thinks about him?"

Julie stared at him, her mouth set, her expression closed and defensive. "I don't think you're an expert on this subject, Nick."

Nick pursed his lips and let out a long breath, then shook his head and reached for the check. "What about Danielson?" he asked abruptly.

Julie blinked at the change of subject. "What about him?"

"When does he ride?"

She made a pretense of casually flipping a page on her clipboard to scan the roster. The show of indifference probably didn't fool Nick. "Fifteenth."

"We selling free-lance footage of him?"

She was startled into meeting his gaze. "No. He's . . . not local," she said.

"So what? Two to one the blue-eyed cowboy from Montana is the favorite around here anyway. Last year he risked his neck to get some young kid bull rider out of trouble when the guy's hand was caught in the rope. You're the one who came up with that research. He was a hero all over Utah."

"I know," Julie said.

"So?"

She glanced at him warily.

"You schedule an interview with him?"

She flipped the page down. "He hasn't given an interview in fifteen years, Nick. He doesn't like the press. It's not a good idea to go marching up to him and demand an interview."

"What about tiptoeing up to him?" Nick said.

"You've got a general rep for that, kiddo. What about using some of that famous technique?"

She stared at him, feeling her stomach tighten with tension she didn't want to show her sharp-tongued, acerbic partner. "I learned how to use my technique years ago, Nick. I also learned it's a waste of time trying to accomplish miracles. We don't have extra time, as far as I can tell."

"Danielson is prime time," the cameraman said implacably. "Not extra."

She gestured impatiently. "I'm working on it. But his schedule is crazier than ours. He's flying up to Alberta after Reno, then back to pick up his camper and drive to Greeley. I'm not likely to run into him hanging out in the local coffee shop."

"So catch him between rides," Nick suggested. "Buy him a beer. Corner him between the chutes and the stock pens after a rodeo some night."

To Julie's acute discomfort, she felt heat rising up her neck. She couldn't meet Nick's gaze. She took refuge in her coffee mug, burned her tongue, then swore under her breath as hot liquid sloshed onto her hand.

Nick watched the performance in surprise, then assessed the silence. When she put the mug down, he set his own mug on the table and leaned back in his chair.

"What's with you, Fielding?"

She looked up at him.

"If you're having a fling with a cowboy, so much the better. It'll make him more willing to talk to you."

"I'm not having a fling."

"Why not?"

"Because it's not my style," she said through gritted teeth.

Nick huffed. "I'll tell you what's not your style, kiddo—backing off from a job. A chance for some controversy, a guy who hasn't given an interview in fifteen years—the Julie Fielding I know would consider that a nice challenge."

She let out a breath.

Nick leaned over the table, burly forearms propped on the edge. "I have a feeling this cowboy's going to take the title this year. If we've got exclusive tape when he does, you can name your next job, Julie—program director or whatever you want, all the way up to station manager."

Julie swallowed, her eyes on her mug.

"I can get him in the ring, but you've got to get him outside of it. If he won't do it for the camera, take the mikes and get him on audio. We'll do a voice-over. But we need an interview. What he thinks about winning, about losing . . . about his time in the slammer. Get it."

"Get him to talk about his time in the slammer," Julie echoed. "You don't ask for much, do you?"

There was a moment of silence.

Julie met Nick's steady gaze, then nodded once and stared down at the table.

"No arguments?" he asked.

"No point in arguing when you're right," she told him.

He leaned away from the table and gave her a smug grin. "Smart woman. You'll do it, then?"

She tipped her head and ran her fingers through her hair. "Of course I'll do it," she told him. "It's part of the job, isn't it?"

Late morning sunlight, hazy with earlier rain, slanted across the nearly empty rodeo grounds.

Julie sat on a bench in the shadow of the announcer's booth, watching Tanner Danielson on a dappled gelding. He rode toward the center of the ring, then leaned down to gesture and say something to a boy who couldn't have been more than fifteen. The youngster had been thrown three times already. Each time he'd got himself up, limped back toward the rails, and waited for Tanner to round up the bronc and lead it back into the chute. This time Tanner gestured the boy off the chutes, shook his head at what was obviously a protest, then gave the young bronc rider a satisfied clap on the shoulder and grinned toward an older man, probably a father, sitting on the rails.

Julie watched the boy slap his hat more securely onto his head and return Tanner's thumbs-up. Fifteen. He could have been the young cowboy Skye had been calling. Julie's mouth tightened. When had Skye become preoccupied with cowboys? Or interested in having a boyfriend? She'd hardly mentioned either subject before the documentary came up.

Julie herself hadn't been interested in boys until she was . . . what? Fifteen? Fourteen?

She shut off the troubling thought, pushed herself up from the bench, and climbed the weathered gray rails in front of her to hitch her elbows over the top. Climbing the rails was an adolescent urge indulged by every kid who got the chance, and the action, usually forbidden for safety reasons, offered childish and uncomplicated satisfaction. Her knees bumped the lower rail, and Julie hooked her leg through it, one foot dangling inside the fence.

From across the arena Tanner caught sight of her and shifted in the saddle. He nodded at the man he'd been speaking to and rode toward her. She swung herself up to perch on the top rail, fighting a curious, exhilarating lift that went back half her life: the cowboy you liked riding toward you while you propped your hands beside your hips on the rails and tried to look casual.

It was impossible to forget that he'd kissed her the last time she'd seen him. Impossible not to remember the feel of his shoulders, the heat of his body, the way she'd responded to him. Impossible not to wish she hadn't.

He stopped in front of her, pulling up the gelding and resting his hands on the saddle horn. It was clear he hadn't been on a bronc himself. He looked cool, clean, and unwrinkled as he sat on the horse with the easy grace of a born rider. His slow nod of greeting, two fingers to his hat, took in her blue tank top, jeans, and old boots in one appraising sweep.

A smile, slow and amused, curved his mouth. "I didn't realize you'd been watching," he said.

"I didn't realize you'd been giving lessons."

Tanner shrugged, then glanced back toward the chutes. "It wasn't really a lesson," he told her. "Just a few pointers for an old friend's son. He's a nice kid."

Beneath the brim of his hat his eyes roved over her face, lingering for a moment on her mouth. A wave of tingling sensation swept through her. She raised her shoulders, feeling the warmth of the sun across her back, leaned her weight on her arms, and asked, "Is he riding this afternoon?"

"No. He's not ready yet. He might be pretty good at it someday though. What do you think?"

It wasn't what she thought that mattered, Julie reflected wryly. It was what she felt and what

Tanner did to her that made it so damn hard to remember she was here to do a job.

"I think the whole sequence should have been taped in Nick's camera. I was wishing he was here."

Tanner tipped his head down, half-smile hidden by his hat. "I'm not sure young John would appreciate that."

"Why not?" she challenged him. "Nobody gets on a bronc and stays on the first time. There's nothing wrong with being thrown. Why object to anyone's seeing it?"

"I don't know, Jule." He leaned forward. "There's nothing wrong with a lot of things you don't necessarily want to do in public. Seems to me you have personal experience with that."

It was a blatant reference to the kiss they'd shared behind the stock pens, and she couldn't pretend not to understand it. But it wasn't a reference she was going to pursue. She was here to get an interview, she reminded herself. To do a job.

"The project we're working on will center around the top few contenders," she said coolly. "We'll pick three or four of them ultimately, and then focus on them for the few weeks we're on the circuit. It will be more biographical then anything else—how they live, what they think, what they have to *say*. Not just how they ride."

He adjusted his hat. "Yeah," he muttered, noncommittal.

"That's what rodeo's about, Tanner. The people in it. It's not just a few winning rides on videotape."

His gaze swept up from her boots, lingering a moment at her tank top, to her face again. "I guess you know as much about it as I do, Jule."

She let out a breath, exasperated that he wouldn't cooperate in her attempt to keep this conversation on business. "But nobody out there wants to hear what a reporter from Seattle knows about it. They want it from a cowboy."

"Yeah?" Tanner grinned, and Julie mentally kicked herself for the unintentional wording. "That true for you too?" he said.

His tone of voice was impudent, teasing, and cowboy-arrogant, and it sent a small flutter of heat from her knees to the top of her head. She didn't trust the flutter, any more than she trusted Tanner. Her errant gaze flickered toward his mouth, and the answer to his question hovered in the air between them like forbidden smoke.

She made herself grin as if she hadn't got the reference. "Anyone would have a hard time pinning you down long enough to talk to, Tanner. How many rides have you had in the past two days?"

"I'm not riding tonight," he said. The corners of his mouth drifted down with seriousness.

"No?" The catch in her voice wasn't quite covered by the smooth question.

"You want to let me buy you dinner?"

She shook her head. "Dinner goes on the company, Tanner."

"Not where I was thinking of taking you."

She shouldn't pursue it, she knew, but she heard herself asking, "Where's that?"

"My place."

Insinuations twined with her thoughts like tangleweed, chased by warnings that tightened her hands around the rails as if she could hold herself to earth. "I've . . . got a partner to answer to, Tanner. I'm working. We've got a rodeo tonight."

"Tell him you're interviewing me. Bring your tape recorder."

She gazed at him, taken off guard by what could have been either blunt honesty or teasing amusement. "And am I? Interviewing you?"

He studied her a moment, then nodded, unsmiling, although mischief shone in his eyes. "You want it from a cowboy, Jule, I reckon you can have it."

She swallowed, not trusting her voice, then settled for a simple nod.

"Third camper from the end, south side of the contestants' parking lot," Tanner said. He touched his hat again, lifted the reins, and nudged his horse into a canter, back toward the chutes, leaving Julie wondering if she'd just pulled a professional coup or been taken in by a come-on.

She decided to regard it as a professional coup as she made her way toward Tanner's camper in the waning sunset light that spilled unevenly across the parking lot. She stepped over a temporarily rigged electrical hookup, paused a moment outside the third camper from the end, and squared her shoulders inside her white T-shirt and batik print jumper.

Get him to talk about his time in the slammer, she and Nick had agreed. Get it on tape. She let out a breath and knocked on the metal door.

The knob turned, and the door opened outward toward her. "Hi," Tanner said from the doorway.

"Hi. I guess I found you."

"I guess you did."

His pale yellow, silver-snapped shirt and near-new jeans said *cowboy,* as did his courtesy of stepping down in front of her, holding the door, and waiting for her to go in ahead of him. Conscious of him behind her, Julie climbed the two steps into the compact quarters of Tanner's home.

It reflected Tanner's rootlessness and rodeo glory in a way she recognized immediately—from the faded bandanna hanging on the mirror to the silver belt-buckle trophies that testified to winning rides and the saddle slung over the back of the passenger seat.

The smell of cayenne peppers and onions wafted from a pot bubbling on the two-burner stove, and snapshots covered the camper's wood-paneled walls—portable tokens of permanence that were standard in rodeo life. She'd never seen a cowboy's home without them.

The setting belonged in her documentary, she realized, seeing it for a moment through the eyes of a documentary filmmaker. Nick was right. They needed this: the background, the atmosphere, Tanner himself. On tape. Talking to her.

When she turned around, her expression animated, he was examining her jumper, T-shirt, and sandals with slow, leisurely interest that stopped at her face, then became an easy smile that had nothing to do with the documentary. The comment on Julie's lips died before it was spoken, replaced by a catch in her breath Nick wouldn't have approved of.

"I was wondering if you'd show up wearing jeans and that skinny little tank top, and those old boots," Tanner said.

His look discomposed her. "It wasn't *that* skinny."

He grinned. "When I saw you on the rails this

morning, you looked just like you did when you were a gutsy little eighteen-year-old rebel."

"You weren't close enough this morning to know whether I looked eighteen or not."

Tanner's grin transformed into pensive regard, the change in expression unhurried, intimate. "You look even better now, Jule," he said, as if it were a matter-of-fact observation. "With or without the tank top."

Julie's glance met his for a moment, then dropped to the open V of Tanner's shirt. *So do you.* She didn't speak it, but the words would have come readily if she'd let them. The dark hair falling over his forehead was a little shorter than it had been in the photographs, his shoulders a little wider, but the way he used his body was the same—easy athlete's grace and balance, a suggestion of masculine sensuality that made her aware that simply Tanner's way of moving would have identified him to her.

She realized her shoulders were raised, her hands bunched into fists in her pockets, her thoughts straying in the same way that had got her into trouble behind the stock pens. Consciously she relaxed her shoulder muscles. Tanner Danielson held a dangerous attraction for her. She couldn't deny it. But the bottom line was, she was here to do a job, to deliver on Nick's expectations—and her own.

"Tanner, I brought the tape recorder," she said. "I . . . maybe I should get it out, and we can start on some questions."

He didn't argue, and Julie didn't push her luck. She moved to the padded bench where she'd dropped her bag, and pulled out the machine and a mike. The table was already set for two, with heavy white crockery that looked as though it wouldn't break on a rough road, plastic-handled spoons, and mismatched napkins. She'd been invited for dinner, she recalled—and whatever else Tanner might have come to expect after their last encounter. She could feel the heat of that thought low in her body, warming her in spite of her resistance to it.

She moved one of the settings to put down her equipment, plugged in the mike cord, and punched the Record button, then glanced up at the snapshots on the wall and froze, with a small shock of recognition.

"Hey"—she gave him a smile that quickly faded—"this is . . . me."

In a black-and-white eight-by-ten photograph mounted above the table, she was sitting on the rails, smiling at the camera, looking more reckless and unburdened and devil-may-care than she ever remembered feeling, even back then.

Beside the photo were more pictures of the same vintage: Buck and Tanner leaning against a battered pickup. Buck holding a trophy, Julie, again, in the boots she'd worn that morning, hamming a ride on a saddle thrown over a sawhorse. She'd been laughing at Buck's sullen mood after a loss, threatening to take his place. Tanner had snapped the picture while Buck scowled.

"Yeah." He stepped up behind her in the close confines of the camper.

Julie glanced at him over her shoulder, then gestured self-consciously toward the pictures again, trying to explain the unexpected allure of memories she thought had been entirely unwanted. "I mean, all of these from . . . so many years ago. Me. Buck. All of us. The way it was back then."

"You didn't think I'd have pictures?"

"I . . ." She shrugged noncommittally.

"Every cowboy who knew Buck has a picture of him, Jule. Cowboys have long memories for someone who . . . ran out of luck. Almost everybody—riders, stockboys, announcers—they remember him. And you."

"Me?" She made a skeptical sound in the back of her throat, but thoughts of the stockman who'd walked in on the kiss she'd shared with Tanner flickered across her consciousness.

Uncomfortable with the recollection, she pushed her hands deeper into her pockets and shivered as if she were still wearing the tank top that left her shoulders and arms bare.

"Maybe we could . . . start with some questions, Tanner," she murmured, moving a step away from him, turning so that she didn't block the mike.

Tanner's gaze flicked toward it, then back to Julie. The half-resigned, half-amused lift to his eyebrows let her know he was aware of her discomfort.

She pulled her hands out of her pockets and made herself relax, gathering her thoughts, aware that the process should be easier than this. She might as well start in the middle, she decided ironically. That was where she always seemed to be with Tanner anyway.

"Tell me what you think about being Cowboy of the Year," she said finally. "About winning the title."

"Winning'd be fine with me." He bent at the waist and opened the refrigerator door, then brought out two cans of beer and popped the top of one. "Would you like a beer?"

She took the offering.

"Glass?"

"No thanks," she told him. "Do you think you'll do it?"

"Do what?"

"Win the title."

"I couldn't say."

Julie touched the side of her neck, watching Tanner, taking a sip of beer, considering how to take charge of this interview. It was just a matter of preparation, and being concerned about what the subject had to say. She was covered on both counts.

"Do you care?" she asked him softly.

He studied her. "Yeah." He drank from his can, and she returned his look with practiced patience, letting the silence stretch out a little. After a moment he said, "Been a long time since I cared whether anyone watched me ride, Jule."

She didn't follow up on the implication in his softly spoken words. Carefully she lowered her beer until it rested on her hip. Conscious of the machine, and how Nick would soon be listening to the tape, she made her voice level. "Since your prison time?"

Tanner's gaze was just as level as her voice. "That's not the connection."

"I suppose I don't have any reason to think it would be," Julie said truthfully. "But I guess I wanted to bring it up anyway." She let her eyes meet his and said softly, "I know it was important to you, that it changed you. You don't serve a jail sentence without being affected by it."

"At the time," he said evenly, "you didn't seem much interested, Jule."

Not interested? She got a quick image of herself, pregnant, sitting on the foldout sofa bed in her tiny apartment, one of Tanner's letters clutched in her fist and her emotions frayed beyond endurance. Interested didn't begin to cover her feelings. She'd been scared, alone, desperate. Too close to unraveling to answer him.

"I'm . . . interested now, Tanner," she said finally.

The blue eyes studied her with such intensity that she felt as if it were a touch. "In what?"

"What it was like. What you did."

"I rode for the prison team. And I sat in a cell I never expected to be in."

"What does a man think about, sitting in a cell, doing time he never expected to do?"

His grin was a little cynical. "Beer. Women. Freedom."

"The girl you went to jail for?"

He looked up, his expression serious, with some kind of subtle challenge in it. "I guess you could say that." He glanced past her, toward the photographs on the wall, and Julie followed his gaze. The picture he was looking at was the one of her on the rails.

Five

Frowning, puzzled, she regarded him uneasily as the tape recorder hissed in the silence and Julie's confused thoughts chased themselves around her head. "What was her name?" she said finally.

Tanner frowned back at her.

"The Mexican girl?"

He tipped his head down and rubbed the back of his neck with one hand. "I don't remember," he said finally.

He didn't remember?

He shifted his weight forward and turned away from her. She recognized the body language that told her he didn't want to pursue this line of conversation, and she expected him to break it off with some meaningless action, like checking the pot on the stove, but instead he reached for one of the belts looped around a wall hook.

Julie gripped her beer can, thinking that an interview with Tanner would always involve fighting for answers that would have come naturally with any other subject, and aware, with another part of her mind, that this conversation had gone beyond the realm of an interview.

Tanner's thumb brushed over the engraved silver of the buckle as Julie watched. When he looked up at her, the intensity of his glance made the muscles of her stomach tighten. "Buck was the one who got the harsh sentence, didn't he? It could have been Buck in jail, me on that bull. That's how I used to feel when I was doing time. Sorry. Guilty. Guilty that I was the one riding, and Buck was dead."

"You didn't have anything to feel guilty about, Tanner," she said too quickly, then stopped the rush of words before she could say anything more. She'd very nearly said, *We didn't have anything to feel guilty about.*

The thought shocked her, and she tried to push it back without examining it. *We.* There hadn't been any *we.* She and Tanner had never betrayed Buck with so much as a word or a touch. What would they have had to feel guilty about?

He hung the belt back on the hook, beside all the other rodeo accoutrements, pieces of his life, pieces of a lifestyle she'd once lived.

The movement pulled his shirt taut against his chest. The silver snaps strained, then eased as he dropped his arm. The thought of his taped ribs—and the lean, muscled torso behind the tape—set off a shower of conflicting feelings in Julie: familiarity overlaid with the acute consciousness that she'd never seen him without a shirt; the old resentment she'd felt when she'd lived on the rodeo circuit; and the strong, seductive attraction this man held for her, stronger even than the giddy tumult of emotion that had made her follow Buck into the crazy, untenable life of a rodeo cowboy.

The pull of opposing feelings set her nerves taut with tension. He made no move to step away after he hung the belt. He stood too close, his gaze intent and probing, while seconds ticked by and Julie felt her heart hammering.

It could have been me on that bull. It still could, she thought, with a strange, queasy wave of panic.

She pressed a palm against the side of her neck and closed her eyes for a moment.

Tanner's fingertips touched the back of her hand. A shock of warmth sang all along the nerves in her arm, and she opened her eyes to meet his blue, steady gaze. His fingers threaded with hers, cupping her hand, his thumb just brushing her cheek.

"Logic doesn't have much to do with it, Julie," he said. "I'd think you'd know that by now." The corners of his mouth curved up, and she watched, fascinated, as her throat went dry and the bottom dropped out of her stomach.

She wanted him to kiss her. She wanted him to step closer to her, touch his lips to hers, give her permission to kiss him back, explore the taste and texture and heat of his mouth. . . .

She moved out from between Tanner and the table and took a shaky step away from him, ignoring the trembling of her hands and the fluttering in her stomach. She lowered her beer to the table, afraid she'd drop it.

He didn't move closer, or touch her again. Julie turned around to find him still a step away, his thumbs tucked into the waistband of his dark blue jeans. "What'd I say?"

"Nothing. I just"—she shook her head—"haven't thought about things from your point of view—

what your life might have been like, what you've been doing."

He shrugged. "Why should you?"

"I'm a reporter. That's what I'm supposed to do."

"Come on, Jule."

"I seem to have a hard time doing that with you, Tanner. I seem to be stuck somewhere in 1980, like I've walked back into it and nothing's changed." Without warning her eyes started to burn, and she felt a lump rise in her throat. She swallowed hard, disgusted with herself, and covered her eyes with one hand.

Tanner didn't move until she'd lowered her hand. Then he gripped her shoulders and leaned toward her. "I don't know about 1980, Jule. I don't know if I'm stuck there or not. Maybe I am. Maybe it doesn't matter."

"I think it does, Tanner."

His hands moved down her arms, then slipped back up to her shoulders inside the sleeves of her T-shirt. "Yeah, maybe it does," he murmured, his voice gruff. "We could find out. . . ."

Her protest was as meaningless as his agreement. He pulled her lightly against him and touched his mouth to hers, gently and without haste, as if there were no question that she'd accept the kiss.

Without question, she did. Her lips opened, and her tongue flicked out to meet his with heart-stopping intimacy.

Tanner slid his hands across her back inside her T-shirt, his palms flat against her bare skin, warm as the sun she'd felt that morning. His fingertips pressed against the hollows at the base of her neck. Sensuous shivers chased down her spine, and she let herself explore his mouth with her kiss, let her hands circle his body, just below the tape that protected his rib cage.

His fingers massaged the back of her head, tipping it to fit their mouths more closely together as his hot, wet tongue explored the intimate surface of her lips, slipped inside again to plunder and possess before he withdrew to nibble at the corner of her mouth.

She turned her mouth to his, seeking and demanding the full pressure of his kiss, and with a muffled groan Tanner gave it. He gathered her fully against him, while one hand grasped her shoulder, then stroked down the length of her arm, her hip, her thigh. He slid his hand upward, pushing the material of her dress with it, then his warm palm cupped the back of her leg beneath her skirt. His fingers splayed on the curve of her buttocks and pulled her flush against him. He was hard and aroused, and beneath the zipper of his jeans the solid ridge of male flesh pressed against her stomach. He drew her leg beside his hip and lifted her to bring the heat of their bodies together.

For a spinning, dizzying span of time, the kiss went on as Tanner moved against her, and Julie found herself responding as she hadn't intended, following his hips with her own in the ancient and unspoken rhythm of assent.

The kiss ended with a slow parting of mouths as Tanner lifted his head. Slowly she opened her eyes, aware of her breathing, rushed and strident as his, of the pulse beating in the hollow of his throat, of his body pressed hard against hers.

He grasped her shoulders, then rested his chin against her forehead while the heat of his body sent messages she was all too ready to receive.

"Stay with me, Jule." His voice was a thick murmur. "I want you to stay all night."

It would have been easy to say yes. She wanted to say it, longed for it with every sensual thought racing through her mind, but beneath the crazy, enticing pleasure she groped for the sensible voice of reason she'd thought of as her real self for thirteen years. For longer than thirteen years. From the time she'd discovered she was pregnant with Skye.

"I . . . can't."

She felt his breath on her hair. "Why not?" he queried gruffly.

"Because I . . ."

His hands tightened around her shoulders. "Because of Buck?"

She shook her head. *Because of Skye* echoed in her mind. "I . . . just can't."

"Jule . . ." His fingers gentled again, moving in slow seductive circles against her skin.

His touch was all too alluring, her resolution all too weak, but she had no chance to test it. The tension between them was abruptly broken by a ringing phone.

Tanner muttered something under his breath, unmoving. At the third ring, Julie tipped her head down farther and said, "I . . . left this number with the motel, Tanner."

She felt his questioning look, then he let go of her to reach for the phone between the bucket seats of the cab.

"Yes," he said into it, then glanced back toward Julie. "It's for you."

"Thanks," She took the receiver from him.

"Ms. Fielding?" the voice on the phone inquired. "Message. From Skye. To call her."

"Thank you," Julie said. "What was—?" But the dial tone clicked on, and the impersonal voice was no longer there. Julie's automatic concern for Skye increased her heartbeat a notch even while she was telling herself it was probably nothing more serious than Skye not being able to find her favorite socks. Still, to ignore the message was impossible. She was Skye's mother. If Skye needed her . . .

She turned back to Tanner. "I . . . have to go."

"That was the station?" he said after a moment.

"No."

Tanner's eyes narrowed with the question he didn't ask.

"Just a . . . personal thing," she said.

Tanner studied her a moment, then stepped toward her, put his hands on her shoulders again, and pulled her close. For a moment he was still, then his hands slid down her back, pressing her against him again. "So take care of it and come back," he said.

She wanted to say yes, to stop fighting the almost unbearable temptation to give in to the needs Tanner aroused in her. She swallowed and squeezed her eyes shut.

Tanner let out a long breath that stirred the hair on the top of her head, then he stepped back from her, slid his hands down her arms, and let her go. "Come back," he said again.

For a moment she had the urge to step into his arms, but the irrepressible voice of reason kept her from doing it. She glanced toward the still-spinning tape recorder, then reached out and snapped it off. She turned away from him to pick up her bag and recorder.

"You could leave all that here," Tanner said.

She hesitated, glanced back at him, then quickly looked away. "Maybe I'd better bring it. I . . . don't like to leave equipment."

She felt a quick tightening of tension and a flash of anger, whether from Tanner or from herself, she couldn't say. When she loaded the bag and turned around, his face was impassive.

He reached for the straps of the bag and slid them up over her shoulder. His fingers lingered for an instant, then he drew back his hand, walked across the small space to the door, and opened it for her.

She brushed by him without saying anything more, silently begging that he not demand whether she was coming back.

He didn't.

Grateful for the respite, Julie stepped down into the parking lot and walked away from him, aware that it was the third time she'd done it.

Each time had been harder.

"Hello?"

The voice on the phone was breezy, casual, and had a sophisticated lilt that made it sound at least three years older than Skye's.

Julie's answering hello came only after a startled pause.

"Oh. Mom," Skye answered. "I've been trying to call you!"

"I got the message," Julie said. "Are you okay, Skye? Did something happen?"

"Oh, no, Mom. It's nothing like that."

Julie felt her shoulders wilt in relief.

"It's just . . ." Skye paused. "Gee, I can't wait till

you get back. When we go shopping, can I get a black rayon top?"

The question was more diversionary tactic than real concern, Julie sensed, but it roused familiar guilt at being away from Skye. "Black rayon?"

"I really need something besides T-shirts, Mom. I don't have anything to wear to . . . like . . . dinner with Rosa's sister."

"Well, maybe you could borrow one of my scarves," Julie suggested.

"Mm."

"What did you call about that couldn't wait, Skye?"

"Well, I . . . sort of had a . . . disagreement with Rosa," Skye admitted. "There's this party, Mom, that I wanted to go to, and Rosa said I couldn't. But I knew if I asked you, you'd say it was okay, and it's not *fair* that Rosa just said no without even asking you! So I told her I was gonna call, and she said—"

"Skye," Julie said sternly, "we've talked about playing Rosa off against me when I'm gone. That's not fair to her or to me and you know it. We agreed on that."

"But Rosa won't let me do anything!"

"Like," Julie said, frowning, "this party?"

"Yeah."

"What kind of party?"

"Well, it's sort of after the school dance. It's at Megan's house, and she's this new girl I'm really good friends with, and Rosa says she doesn't know them, but geez, Mom, if you knew them, you'd like them. They're really nice, and so's—"

"Skye," Julie broke in. "No parties unless I've met the parents."

"But, *Mom* . . ."

"Is this boy you've been calling going to be at the party, Skye?" Julie asked with suspicious insight.

There was a reappraising pause. Skye's silence said *guilty*, but her daughter rallied almost immediately. "You said I couldn't date, Mom. You didn't say I couldn't go to parties."

"How old is the girl giving the party?"

"Sixteen."

Julie digested the information while her stomach tied itself into a knot. "And everyone else there?"

"Are you gonna say they're too old for me?" Skye queried rebelliously.

"Yes."

"You mean *Gary's* too old for me!"

"Yes. He is."

"Well, maybe *he* doesn't think so!"

"Then his judgment is questionable," Julie snapped.

Skye's voice rose in adolescent mutiny. "You're ruining my life! You just want to keep me home all the time because you're not here. But that's not *my* fault! I don't see why I have to be *grounded* just because you have to go off and make some documentary!"

"You're not grounded," Julie told her. "Though you're working on it. But no party. And phone time is still half an hour a day, ten minutes a call. Is that clear? Skye?"

"All right!" Skye's voice, angry and hurt, barked over the phone.

Julie shut her eyes again, feeling her own churning emotions match her daughter's. "I'll be home in a week and a half, Skye."

"Okay." Sullen.

"We'll plan to go shopping, okay?"

"Okay, Mom," Skye said before she handed the phone to Rosa.

Julie hung up five minutes later trying not to feel slighted, and telling herself Skye's rebellion was normal. But she stared at the phone for several seconds after she'd put it down.

So take care of it and come back.

It was out of the question, as she'd known it would be. So why this sudden, swift drop of disappointment?

She squeezed her eyes shut and pressed her palm to her mouth, telling herself to see things in perspective. In a little more than a week she'd be home with Skye, back to her normal life.

Tanner Danielson would be just a memory. A mistake she hadn't made.

An echo of the heat that had flared between them washed through her, like high-noon sun, tempting and heady, and Julie banished it with the discipline of long practice, telling herself the prickle of cold, bleak loneliness was just momentary.

At least she hadn't mentioned Tanner to her daughter. Skye's headlong rush into adolescence was tumultuous enough without the emotionally charged situation of having her mother involved with a man.

A cowboy. Julie let her head drop forward. Who was *she* to tell Skye to be sensible, to go slowly, to be careful not to lose her heart over adolescent urges and the unpredictable demands of blossoming hormones?

A cowboy. Tanner Danielson was as dangerous in his way as the broncs he rode. She'd be better off getting involved with one of the horses.

• • •

"Hey, Danielson!" the stockman called. "Your ladyfriend is down here tellin' all your secrets to the meanest bronc we got!"

Tanner peered toward the voice in the dim afternoon haze of the pens, frowning.

"I wouldn't worry, though," the man called, chuckling. "Seems like Piece O'Cake is partial to blondes."

Tanner swore, turning on his heel and striding across the aisle even while he cursed himself for not walking the other way. She'd said she wasn't interested in life on the road. She didn't want anything personal to do with anyone or anything that was rodeo. Dammit, she'd walked away from him the night before, leaving him with an ache in his jeans and an urge to go out and get blind drunk, which he hadn't done because he'd been fool enough to think she might come back.

So what the hell was she doing hanging around the stock pens with a bronc whose mean streak was wide enough to roll over half of Texas?

"She's mad too." The stockman grinned as Tanner rounded the corner of the crossway. "You'll never ride this bronc again, cowboy." He laughed toward his companion, who touched his hat, and mumbled something indecipherable.

Tanner ignored the joke as well as the mumble, smoothly moved one of the men aside with a hand on his shoulder, and walked toward Julie as if they had a standing appointment to meet in front of Piece O'Cake's pen. She didn't look any friendlier than the bronc.

"Julie," he said, two fingers to his hat.

"Tanner." She glanced toward him, perfectly

still, one foot on the bottom rails, her wrist draped across the top slat of the bronc's pen.

"You looking for me?"

"No. I was looking for the horse," she said.

He took the last step toward her, slid his hand around her waist, and touched her lightly in the center of her back, guiding her away from the pen with a gesture he hoped was too courteous to argue about. She moved, not arguing.

He smiled at the two stockmen. "Excuse us, boys."

One man nodded at Julie. "Sorry about what you heard, ma'am. We didn't know you were there." He shot a *Don't take offense* look at Tanner.

The man with the mouth added his own nod of apology. "Just a little matter of a wager. Cowboys'll bet on anything, you know." He grinned again.

Abashed laughter accompanied their retreat, and Julie stepped away from Tanner's hand and shot him a look that said *humiliated* and *furious* at the same time. She reached for the top rail again.

Tanner caught her wrist before she touched the rail. "Stay away from that horse, dammit! He bites."

She tugged at her wrist. "He hasn't bitten me yet."

"That's no reason to keep trying."

"Let go of me, Tanner."

Fighting an instinct that shocked him with its intensity, he released her wrist and shoved his hands into his pockets. She glared back at him.

After a moment he let out a breath. "Maybe you're having a bad day, Julie, but it won't get better if you get a couple of fingers bitten off."

"I wasn't having a bad day until I ran into the company you keep around here."

Tanner made a mental note to strangle the two stockmen. He knew what they'd probably been betting on. He'd heard the local gossip concerning him and Julie. "So what the hell are you doing here?" he asked tightly.

"Talking to the damn horse!"

His mind went blank for a moment. "You're hanging out in the stock pens talking to the horses," he said, deadpan. "Who gave you that great idea?"

"You did," she said curtly. She folded her arms across her tank top, her weight on one hip as she faced him. "With your comment about how half the score goes to the horse. Maybe one of the bucking horses deserves a profile."

Tanner gritted his teeth. "And you had to pick one with the disposition of a wet rattler who never heard of manners."

"The manners of the *horse* aren't my problem back here."

"Yeah, well," he drawled, "if you're going to hang out behind the chutes—"

"Don't give me that old rodeo saw about women not having any business behind the chutes, Tanner! I'm a reporter. I have a job to do, and I don't need a lot of heat from you or anyone else about it."

He felt a rush of temper and throttled it while she turned one shoulder to him. She was right, and the anger he felt didn't have much to do with women behind the chutes. Or what careers they committed themselves to. "I don't give a damn about your job," Tanner said deliberately.

She took a deep breath, raised her head, and stared at the far wall. "I don't expect you to give a damn about my job," she said with that cool distance that made him want to move in close enough to see the pulse in her neck throb. "I'll do that." She risked a look at him.

"Where were you last night?" he said softly.

She dropped her gaze, but not before her eyes caught his and he saw a flicker of awareness that moved through her like a faint shiver.

"I . . . something came up," she said lamely.

He stared at her for a long moment, accusation replacing the skepticism in his gaze as seconds ticked by and she offered no more honest explanation. "Something so important you couldn't call back?" he said finally, sarcasm thick in his voice.

She closed her eyes and threaded her fingers through the hair at the nape of her neck. "Important enough." After a minute she looked at him again. "I didn't come back because it wasn't a good idea, Tanner."

"You could have said that."

"I didn't need to say it," she flared. "You knew it. And you knew I might not come back. All right, I should have called you, but I—"

"Couldn't get away?" he said shortly. *From what? Or who?*

"I'm sorry," she said defiantly. "I should have called you, okay? I didn't think a call would make much difference."

Tanner let out a huff of resignation, while one corner of his mouth turned up mirthlessly. "No, I guess not. If you can think of something I wanted to do last night with a *phone*, you've got a better imagination than I do, honey."

She turned away from him, reached for the top rail of the stock pen, and leaned her forehead against it.

Tanner grabbed her shoulders and yanked her back. A split second later the metal slats clanged against the chain link as Piece O'Cake kicked the gate, rattling the chains viciously.

Tanner, one arm clamped around her shoulders, the other around her waist, held her tightly against the length of his body. His mouth next to her ear, he said, "Stay away from the pen, *lady*. What the hell do you think you're dealing with here?"

Julie's heart was hammering, and she swallowed. The question hung in the charged atmosphere, heavy with irony and slightly strained humor. *What did she think she was dealing with?* Pressed against Tanner's body, her backside in intimate contact with that part of his she'd responded to so blatantly the night before, she had little doubt what she was dealing with: a healthy, willing, virile male who had made no secret of what he wanted, whose overtures she had answered with elemental passion, and whose bed she had deserted with no reason or excuse.

Because no reason or excuse would have held against the temptation she'd felt to go back to it.

"All right," she said, her voice strained. "I'll stay away from the pen."

She felt his breath against the side of her neck, then his hold on her loosened, but he brushed his hands up her arms to cup her shoulders in a rough grip.

"You should know better than that, Julie," he said, his voice rough with the effort of trying to sound normal. "You've been around rodeo for too many years to start acting like you can trust the bucking stock."

"I haven't been around rodeo all these years," she said, trying to ignore what his touch did to her.

He didn't answer for a moment, and she felt his struggle to make his voice level. When he spoke, he had won the battle. His words were quiet and confidential. "You remember that time at the bucking-horse sale, you and that crazy girlfriend of yours, Rita, were out in the corral, and you were going to ride one of the horses?"

Her shoulders slumped in surrender to the memory. Yes, she remembered. Buck had been furious that his wife would break the strict, sexist rule that no woman could ride a bronc.

"You would have done it, wouldn't you?" Tanner said, his hands tightening around her shoulders.

"Maybe so," Julie muttered. A smile touched her mouth. "But by the time I'd finished arguing with Buck, you'd already roped the only one worth trying."

"I didn't want to watch you break your neck."

Silence hung in the air for a moment, then Tanner made a sound in the back of his throat that acknowledged the callousness of the comment.

"Rita had a crush on you," she said, wanting to dissipate Tanner's discomfort with the unwitting reference to Buck's death.

"Rita had a crush on every cowboy who ever won a ride."

"Maybe she wanted to ride herself."

"Maybe she did. I watched the all-women's rodeo once. They weren't bad." His hands moved on her shoulders, and she was electrified by the sexy appeal of his teasing voice. "Considering."

"That's a typical cowboy thing to say. What's wrong with women's rodeo?"

"I didn't say there was anything was wrong with it. What's wrong with cowboys?"

"Nothing." She shrugged. "Nothing. But I . . ."

"But what?"

But they make lousy fathers. She bit her lip to keep from blurting out the thought. It brought a baggage train of old emotions: the desperation she'd felt at being pregnant and alone; the pride that kept her from asking anyone's help because she couldn't bear to hear *I told you so;* the bitter self-blame that was the legacy of her own mistakes and her own failure.

As Tanner combed his fingers into her hair, his forearms pulled her back against him. A hint of challenge was in the action, along with sensuality half-unleashed and unapologetic. "Then maybe you should just forget it."

"I can't."

"You could have last night," he went on. His words held a hard, relentless suggestion. "Hell, you could have thirteen years ago, if you'd let it happen."

She pulled away from his hands and whirled around to face him. "But I didn't, did I? I wasn't free to do it, and I didn't."

"Not then." His gaze was hard, demanding, and steady, but she could see the increased rhythm in his breathing that betrayed the effect his touch had had on him as well as her. He shoved his thumbs into his waistband and stood with legs widespread, shoulders squared, his posture saying he wouldn't back down from whatever was between them.

Threatened by the truth of his words and by her own feelings, Julie bristled. "You think just because Buck is gone, there's nothing to stop us from hopping into bed together whenever the urge might strike?"

A palette of expressions played across his face: skepticism, consternation, a flicker of desire. "I wasn't figuring on hopping, exactly," he drawled. "I don't know how you planned to get there."

She made a disgusted sound and took a step to move around him. He caught her arm to stop her.

"Okay, Jule," he said, the sarcasm gone. "Maybe I did think that way thirteen years ago. Maybe I figured it this time too. It wasn't any damn secret what I wanted that first night in the bar. You wanted it too. And you sure as hell wanted it last night." He paused. "So what the hell's so wrong with that?"

"I don't go in for instant sex, Tanner."

"Thirteen years isn't exactly instant."

"That's not—" She broke off, pulling at her arm.

"Well, what is the point, dammit?"

Her lips thinned into a stubborn line. "I don't have to explain anything to you!"

"No, you sure as hell haven't done that. Every time you let your guard down you let me know you want to be touched. Every time I do it, you light up like fireworks. Then you back away and run like a branding iron's after you. And you throw Buck in my face like you're not sure he died yet."

"*Everything* about him didn't die, Tanner." She stared at him, angry and on the verge of telling him about that part of Buck and her and their flawed marriage that was very much alive, but Tanner's cold gaze raked down her body to her hips, then flicked to her left hand.

"You're not still wearing his ring, Julie, and I don't know if you still would be even if he were alive. If you decided to get honest about it, you'd admit that. You and Buck didn't have a snowball's chance in hell, no matter what tricks you dreamed up to pretend otherwise."

Stung by an accusation that hit a raw nerve, Julie let her temper flare. "And you didn't have any interest in seeing that we stayed together, did you?"

Tanner's mouth was hard. "You want me to admit to that? Okay, yeah, I wanted you thirteen years ago. And yeah, there were times I wished Buck was out of the picture. Not the way it happened, but I wished it. If that's a crime, I've already paid for it."

"So what do you want to do? Cash in?" she spouted bellingerently, defensive and bitter because she was afraid of the temptation she felt to match his honesty, to let go of her pride, and—God help her—to fall for him the way she had once fallen for Buck.

He dropped her arm. "I may be just a cowboy, Julie, but I don't trade on the past. I'm not the one who came waltzing into that bar a couple of weeks ago looking for a cozy little chat about old times so I could put it on videotape and impress some hotshot cameraman who thinks he can make a killing on it. So just who's cashing in on old debts, *lady*?"

As if to emphasize the last word, the horse kicked, his hooves smashing the slats of the pen behind Julie.

Tanner's glance shot toward the pen, and his fist clenched in an obvious effort not to yank her farther away from danger. When he looked back at her, his temper was reined in with iron control, and his voice was hard and tight. "I'd be obliged, *ma'am*, if you'd leave the stock pens to the cowboys who have a job to do here." He pulled his hat lower on his head. "So I'll see you out."

"I can find my own way," she muttered, but Tanner stepped behind her and put his hand on her back. Head high, jaw clenched, she felt like a prisoner being walked to the squad car.

The men working the pens stayed out of her way, but she had little doubt they'd been privy to everything that had gone on, including who was sleeping with whom, or not.

They had twenty-five dollars riding on it.

Six

Nick stared at her as if she'd just tried to sell him the Brooklyn Bridge.

"Let me get this straight, kiddo. You want to replace Tanner Danielson with a *horse*?"

Heads turned toward them in the press corral. Julie made herself ignore the others as she faced Nick. "I know following one of the broncs is an odd twist, Nick, but it would get across the idea that half the score in a ride is based on the horse's performance, and—"

"It's not the horse idea I'm against, kiddo. It's the one about dropping Danielson. If you think you can sell me that piece of insanity—"

"We always knew we were going to weed out some of the contenders, Nick. He's not the only one we're following."

Nick turned fully toward her, aiming the camera at her, its lens like an accusing third eye. "He's the one who's going to take the title."

"You don't know that! This is rodeo. He might break a leg tomorrow."

Passion awaits you...
Step into the magical world of

Loveswept

A Magical World of Enchantment Awaits You When You're Loveswept!

Your heart will be swept away with Loveswept Romances when you meet exciting heroes you'll fall in love with...beautiful heroines you'll identify with. Share the laughter, tears and the passion of unforgettable couples as love works its magic spell. These romances will lift you into the exciting world of love, charm and enchantment!

You'll enjoy award-winning authors such as Iris Johansen, Sandra Brown, Kay Hooper and others who top the best-seller lists. Each offers a kaleidoscope of adventure and passion that will enthrall, excite and exhilarate you with the magic of being Loveswept.

- ♥ **We'd like to send you 6 new novels to enjoy–<u>risk free!</u>**
- ♥ **There's no obligation to buy.**
- ♥ **6 exciting romances–plus your <u>free gift</u>–brought right to your door!**
- ♥ **Convenient money-saving, time-saving home delivery!**

Join the Loveswept at-home reader service and we'll send you 6 new romances about once a month– <u>before they appear in the bookstore!</u> You always get 15 days to preview them before you decide. Keep only those you want. Each book is yours for only $2.25* That's a total savings of $3.00 off the retail price for each 6 book shipment.

*plus shipping & handling and sales tax in NY and Canada

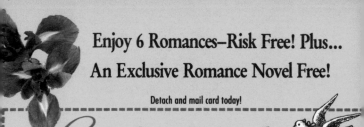

Enjoy 6 Romances–Risk Free! Plus...
An Exclusive Romance Novel Free!

Detach and mail card today!

Loveswept

AFFIX RISK FREE BOOK STAMP HERE.

Yes! *Please send my 6 Love-swept novels RISK FREE along with the exclusive romance novel "Larger Than Life" as my free gift to keep.*

RD 412 28

....

N A M E

....

A D D R E S S   A P T.

....

C I T Y

....

S T A T E   Z I P

MY ''NO RISK''

Guarantee

I understand when I accept your offer for Loveswept Romances I'll receive the 6 newest Loveswept novels right at home about once a month (before they're in bookstores!). I'll have 15 days to look them over. If I don't like the books, I'll simply return them and owe nothing. You even pay the return postage. Otherwise, I'll pay just $2.25 per book (plus shipping & handling & sales tax in NY and Canada). I *save* $3.00 off the retail price of the 6 books! I understand there's no obligation to buy and I can cancel anytime. No matter what, the gift is mine to keep–*free!*

SEND NO MONEY NOW.

♥ 6 Romance Novels–Risk Free! ♥ Exclusive Novel Free!
♥ Money Saving Home Delivery!

FREE BOOK OFFER
RUSH!

BUSINESS REPLY MAIL
FIRST CLASS MAIL   PERMIT NO. 2456   HICKSVILLE, NY

POSTAGE WILL BE PAID BY ADDRESSEE

LOVESWEPT
BANTAM DOUBLEDAY DELL DIRECT
PO BOX 985
HICKSVILLE NY 11802-9827

NO POSTAGE
NECESSARY
IF MAILED
IN THE
UNITED STATES

"Yeah, and if he breaks a leg at the Reno rodeo finals, we get it on tape. And that particular footage would sell the whole project—the cowboy who might have won. Danielson stays. He's the best subject we've got, and you know it."

"Since when? Since when is a hostile subject the best one to follow in a documentary?"

"Hostile?" Nick's eyebrows rose.

"He doesn't want to be interviewed."

"Hostile, my assets," Nick muttered. He snatched a cassette from the case beside him and waved it in her face. "This stuff is dynamite. When you got him talking about how he felt in prison, that was superb. He really opened up there. That part about Buck—"

With a clatter of metal slats, the chute opened, and a rider shot out into the arena. Nick broke off in midsentence and glanced toward the cowboy on the bull, one hand going to his camera, then, after identifying and dismissing the rider, he turned back to her as if he hadn't stopped talking. "And that camper must be a gem, kiddo. We want that camper on tape."

"I can't do it, Nick," she said tightly.

"Bull."

In the ring the bull won. The cowboy hit the dirt, rolled, and scrambled for safety as the rodeo clowns distracted the angry animal and lured him away.

Julie sighed, closing her eyes. "We had an argument, Nick."

She got silence for an answer, and when she opened her eyes to meet his gaze, Nick's mouth curled up in amusement. "I thought there might be some sparks there, with Danielson," he said.

The announcer's voice rasped out the name Nick had just spoken, filling in the blank arena time with patter about Tanner's record of wins, his style, his status in the Reno finals.

Julie's eyelids flickered in reaction to the name, then she turned back to Nick. "It was more than just *sparks*," she said. "He thinks I'm . . . cashing in on old debts." Her lids flickered again, and she burst out, "I can't *use* people, Nick. It's not fair. How can I face my daughter if I can't justify—"

"So that's it?" Nick asked. "How can you face Skye and tell her you've got something going with Danielson?"

Julie's eyes widened. "That's not what I said."

"It's what you meant, though," Nick went on. "You think Skye can't handle it?" He gave a derisive huff. "I'll tell you something, kiddo, Skye's growing up. I've known her for a couple of years now. She's a little precocious, but I'll bet she's gonna handle things just fine." His eyes narrowed, then turned challenging as he nodded once, watching Julie. "I have my doubts, though, about her mother."

Julie felt a rush of color in her face. "What's that supposed to mean?"

"It means you can't handle Danielson because you act like being attracted to a man is akin to drug addiction. Skye may be thirteen years old, but even she could tell you what's wrong with that picture."

The flush drained away, and she felt her chest tighten in reaction. It was a moment before she trusted her voice. "My daughter is not an expert on men," she stated through gritted teeth. "Any more than you're an expert on my attitude, Nick."

The chute was yanked open, and Tanner Danielson, on the back of a bull, burst out into the ring, hat flying, one hand swinging wildly as he clung with the other to the rope around the animal's flanks.

Julie's gaze was riveted to the man and the bull, her heart suddenly pounding so loud, it drowned out the crowd noise, the announcer's voice, the whirring of Nick's camera. Her nails dug into her palms in an effort to control the sudden, breathless rush of adrenaline that sent her heart into her throat. The eight-second buzzer sounded, the crowd roared approval, and the pickup men headed toward Tanner. Grinning, he swung a leg over the twisting bull and jumped free even before the riders reached him.

Julie breathed again as a wash of relief loosened her tight muscles, shot through with equal measures of admiration, the same elation of the crowd around her, and fierce pride at Tanner's accomplishment.

When she turned to Nick, she found him watching her, one eyebrow raised, probing assessment on his shrewd, intelligent face.

He didn't bother to express it.

Tanner turned into the parking lot of the Greeley Saddlery and Supply, glanced toward the store's entrance, then pulled across two parking spaces and stopped there, his eyes glued to the front steps.

Julie Fielding was sitting on the stoop.

In boots and a yellow flowered sundress, elbows on her knees and chin propped on the heel of her hand, she was leaning forward just enough to make the wide strap of her dress slip partway down one smooth, pale shoulder. Her blond hair caught the clear Montana afternoon sunlight and reflected it in tiny, seductive glimmers as she moved her head toward his truck.

She straightened slowly, watching him. The yellow skirt moved against her thighs as she drew her hands back.

Tanner had the sudden, crazy urge to smooth it down again, straighten her shoulder strap, and carry her off to some place private enough to peel the whole dress off her and replace it with his hands. The reaction irritated him even while it raised his temperature a few degrees.

He couldn't for the life of him fathom what she was doing here.

He got out of the truck, slammed the door hard enough to rock the cab, and kept staring at her while he reached into the front seat for his favorite Stetson, now flattened and battered, and pulled his second-best hat lower on his forehead. He was halfway across the parking lot before his brain clicked in that Nick had set him up.

Nick had set them both up.

She didn't move as he approached her, but her face said more clearly than words that she wasn't expecting him.

"Don't tell me," he drawled. "You're waiting for your cameraman, right?"

Her eyes narrowed. "Yes." She glanced down at her watch, then looked back at Tanner, frowning. "He was supposed to meet me here half an hour ago with the equipment to do some shots of the store."

Tanner gave a single bark of humorless laughter and tossed his ruined Stetson onto the stoop beside Julie. "He put one leg of his tripod through my hat," he told her. "Then he insisted on making arrangements with the Saddlery to replace it. And he knew damn well this was the only time I'd be able to get out here."

For a moment she stared blankly at the crushed hat, then her shoulders went rigid and her jaw clenched as she realized what he was saying. She glanced up at Tanner and uttered a quiet, succinct, explicit word he wouldn't have repeated in her presence.

He kicked up an angry geyser of gravel with one heel. "You have a hell of a partner, lady. What kind of a crack-brained idea is this? He bet all his money on it or what?"

Julie closed her eyes for a moment, drew in a breath, then let her shoulders slump. Her dress inched a little farther down.

Behind her a cowboy came out of the store and crossed the porch, his eyes flicking toward Julie. He went by her down the stairs, head turning to give her an interested once-over. Tanner's steely glance kept him moving toward the parking lot, but Julie didn't so much as notice him.

She turned a candid, steely gaze on Tanner. "No. He bet his professional tactics on it," she said flatly. "He wants me to get you on tape."

Tanner's hand dropped to his side.

"Video," she told him, in that same tightly controlled voice. "He wants you to go on videotape and tell all the details of when you were in prison. He thinks I can convince you to do it. I'm supposed to use my famous technique or my feminine wiles or something to get you to talk." She glanced away from him, disgusted. "I told him it wouldn't work, but apparently he didn't believe me."

Tanner studied her averted face, letting out a long breath. *Like hell it wouldn't work*. And Nick Johnson, the miserable lowlife, knew that. "He made you drive out here on the chance that I'd show up to be interviewed?"

"Oh, it's worse than that. He got someone to drop me off here. I don't have transportation back. He figured you'd have to offer a ride."

Tanner bit off a curse.

"Well, I'm sorry, all right? It's not my fault. I wouldn't have agreed to it, if I'd known what he was doing. I know you don't . . . owe me anything." Her voice fell on the last words to a low, resigned murmur, and she rested her elbow on her knee again and tilted her forehead into her hand.

Her blond hair hung on either side of her hand, exposing the back of her neck—smooth, soft, somehow vulnerable.

He fought a swift battle with himself, knowing before it started what the outcome would be. It was stupid, and he knew it. One touch and he'd be all over her like wet rawhide.

And halfway through the process she'd get up and walk away, cowboy, he reminded himself, his jaw clenched. But the honesty with which she'd told him Nick's plans defeated his resistance before it started.

Nick Johnson deserved a swift kick in the camera lens for this caper, Tanner promised himself. And he'd get in another one on Julie's behalf too. "Come on," he said gruffly.

She raised her head. "It's not necessary, Tanner."

"*Come on*." He reached down to pick up his

battered hat, and put a hand under Julie's elbow to help her up.

She stood. The yellow dress fluttered around the top of her boots. Glancing down at her, he could see the shadow between her breasts.

"Let's go."

She resisted the slight pressure on her elbow. "Look, don't you want to replace your hat? I think Nick owes you that much."

"I've got other damn hats," he growled.

Julie's eyes took in his scowl in silence. She hitched her bag over her shoulder and shifted her weight back toward the store as if not sure whether to go with him or stay.

The store's owner, a big mixed-blood Crow with a shock of gray hair, appeared in the doorway, watching the exchange that was taking place on his porch, and nodded toward them. His gaze, moving from Julie to Tanner, was genial, but a trace of disapproval was in his voice when he spoke. "This the cowboy been keepin' you waiting for the better part of an hour?"

"No," Julie said quickly, as if defending him.

Tanner yanked his hat farther down on his forehead and made no comment.

The man nodded, his gaze shifting to Tanner's crushed Stetson. "You here to replace that? Got a good selection inside."

"I'll check it out some other time," Tanner told him.

"We got lots of hats," the store owner suggested. His gaze flicked to Julie's hair.

Tanner followed it. "The lady doesn't wear hats," he said, when Julie made no move to answer. "She's not a cowgirl."

Slightly startled brown eyes met his, and at his

increased pressure on her elbow, she walked beside him to the truck.

He opened the door, handed her in, and closed it without speaking.

Halfway back to town, Tanner's hands unclenched from the steering wheel to rub some of the tension out of the back of his neck. He hadn't exchanged a word with Julie since leaving the parking lot. Tanner didn't trust his language. Hell, he didn't trust anything about himself when he was this close to Julie. And the fact that Nick had been betting—probably literally—that his partner would cooperate in the plan infuriated him.

He put his hand back on the steering wheel. *Who're you kidding, Danielson? You're infuriated that she won't. Even when she wants to. Even when she's close enough for you to hear her pulse racing just under that lovely skin.*

Damn every sneaking, lowlife excuse for a newsman who ever covered a rodeo.

Up the road ahead of him was a turnoff onto a narrow dirt path that led through scattered cottonwoods and willows along the canyon bed of a slow stream. Tanner downshifted, slowed the truck, and took the turn.

Julie didn't break the silence between them, but her eyes questioned him when he glanced toward her.

"Mind if we take the long way back?" he asked. "If I run into Nick Johnson right now, I'll regret what I'll do to him."

Her mouth curved, then straightened. "I'm not in a position to object, Tanner."

Whether to the detour or to his plans for Nick, she didn't specify, but his blood heated at the idea of Julie Fielding with him on an unspecified mission, *not objecting.* Her face was turned toward the rocky bluffs at the opposite side of the stream. She had one elbow on the window frame, her hand trailing out the open window.

Is that what he'd wanted? Julie Fielding alone with him, in a place where she couldn't walk away?

A strand of hair blew across her face and caught on her lips. She brushed at it in a slow, unconsciously seductive gesture that fed the tightening in his body.

He wrenched his gaze away.

"Aren't you scheduled to ride this afternoon?" Julie asked him, breaking into his unrewarding thoughts.

"Yeah," he said.

The camper's tires crunched on the gravelly road, counterpoint to the murmuring stream. "What happens if you don't show?"

With effort he kept himself from looking at her again. "They won't let me ride next year. And they give this year's prize to someone else. There's no shortage of cowboys at a rodeo."

"You really don't care about winning, do you?" she asked after a moment.

The way she said the words struck him as honest and . . . personal. He glanced at her, then turned his eyes front again. *Or maybe it's just what you want to hear, Tanner.* "It's a rodeo," he said gruffly. "It's not the end of the world if I don't show."

She didn't say anything, and it made him aware of how much he wanted to hear the sound of her voice, telling him something truthful, something that mattered to her.

So why the hell didn't you say something civil? he sniped at himself.

On the other hand, his inner voice sniped back, maybe it wouldn't make any difference. Maybe she just doesn't want to be here. Maybe she wants to be back on duty, working with tricky Nicky and feeding smooth, salable words into her mike.

He let out a breath, mulling over the possibility that maybe being back at her job was more of a priority for Julie than driving down the south fork of Beaver Creek while he was driving himself nuts into the bargain.

He pulled to a stop on the gravel bank beside the stream, staring out the windshield at the narrow road and acknowledging his own reluctantly noble thoughts. If he did a seventeen-point turn and considered the problem with his brain instead of his jeans, he could get the camper headed back toward town.

"I guess some people care too much about winning, Tanner," she finally said in that soft, slightly husky voice that stroked every masculine nerve in his body.

He glanced toward her.

"Nick does. Making this documentary is everything to him."

"Yeah," he got out. It sounded sarcastic, and Tanner knew the tone was pure self-defense. His resentment of Nick Johnson was real, but it was a damn small part of what was really on his mind.

"I guess I've cared too much about winning too," she said unexpectedly, her voice low but with a conviction that caught his attention and riveted it on her words. "I mean about the documentary." She drew a breath that was a barely audible rasp.

She was staring down at her lap, her face pensive, but with a hint of determination in the line of her jaw. "It's hard to keep it in perspective," she said. "Everything I've done has been working for some kind of security." She smiled briefly, still not looking at him. "It's not the kind of thing you probably think about much. But I . . . needed it, Tanner. I still need it. Still . . ." The brown eyes met his, determined, candid, and with an impact he felt directly in his gut. "It doesn't give me the right to trade on old debts. So I'm sorry. I won't do it again, whatever Nick thinks he can con me into."

At the strained, slightly ragged sigh that ended the statement, Tanner clenched his hands around the steering wheel and swallowed hard. Every instinct urged him to reach for her, pull her into his arms, tell her she could trade on any debts she wanted to as long as they involved one man, one woman, and something beyond words. But he knew if he touched her this time, he'd never have the strength to let her walk away. The need he felt in his gut was raw and hard to fight. He kept his face turned toward the windshield, so he wouldn't see the sweet, vulnerable curve of her jaw, the way her hand slid under her hair when she felt uncertain, the candid, gut-wrenching spark of honesty in her eyes.

The sound of her door opening surprised him into looking at her. She got out of the truck, slammed the door, and stood with her back to him, her spine straight with injured pride, her face turned toward the steep bluffs.

She thought he wouldn't accept her apology, he realized suddenly. Cursing himself, he slammed out of the camper, strode around the front of it, then paused two feet away from her. "Julie . . ."

Her hands were pushed deep into her pockets, shoulders hunched. "It's beautiful here," she said, lifting her eyes to the distant mountains, now deepening to gray-blue in the late afternoon light.

"Yes," he said after a moment, swallowing to keep down the sound of pure desire that had crept into even that single word.

"I forgot that. You wouldn't think it would be so easy to forget that, would you?"

"Yeah, well, memory's a funny thing. And you're not from around here."

"No, that's right." He caught the edge of a grim smile. "I'm not a cowgirl." The late afternoon sun, slanting across the cottonwoods from the mountains, turned her hair to luminous gold and edged her cheek with light. "I've been trying for thirteen years to prove that," she said. "And in the process I forgot all the good things about it. The thing is . . ." She hesitated. "It hurts to remember."

"I know," Tanner said. At the rough emotion in his words, she turned toward him, surprised, her lips slightly parted, as if he hadn't said what she expected.

"Yes, I guess you must," she said. "Buck was a friend of yours."

"So were you."

Slowly, tentatively, she turned partway toward him. "Tanner . . ." She shook her head a little, gave a tiny shrug. The shoulder strap of her dress slipped, and she moved it back with the finger of one hand, then made a small gesture toward him.

Her gaze met his, and the blaze of fierce expression stopped her where she was.

"Don't do that, Jule," he muttered, the words a

rough warning. "Not if you're planning to walk away again."

She went still for a moment, her hand pressed against the side of her neck, her eyes watching him. "I don't think I was," she said.

Seven

Eyes wide, Julie watched Tanner move toward her with one slow, deliberate step. He lifted one hand to her hair. His knuckles brushed back an errant strand, then grazed the curve of her shoulder and traced the strap of her dress.

"This is your idea of work clothes?" he said gruffly, the corners of his mouth turned up.

A tiny shiver rippled along her nerve endings. She watched his gaze drift down to the bodice of her dress, over the swell of her breasts. His eyes moved back up to her shoulder, to her hand, still tucked beneath her jaw, to her face. "I'm the talent for the interview," she said. "I'm supposed to look western and outdoorsy." The sentence caught in her throat and stumbled out on a breath of emotion that had nothing to do with the words.

Tanner's smile faded, and his fingers dipped again toward the curve of her breast. "You have skin like no cowgirl I ever met, Jule. Like the sun never touched it."

He lifted a finger to her face and ran it down the

side of her cheek. Out of the corner of her eye she could see the blur of his hand, dappled under the patch of sun that played over the side of her face and her shoulder, belying what he'd just said. The sunlight felt cool, dry, and ephemeral, while his touch was warm and real and desired.

His eyes dropped from hers to linger for a moment on her shoulder. Then he leaned down toward her, pushing her strap aside as he replaced it with his mouth.

The kiss heated her to the core of her being. Tanner's warm, strong hands closed around her shoulders, pulling her closer, and Julie reached for him, hooking her fingers around his bent elbows.

He smelled of soap, saddle leather, and a dry, elusive trace of rodeo dust, a mixture of scents that was a harbinger of home, remembered, loved, sought after.

He turned to press his open lips against the side of her neck, and Julie murmured his name, stretching her neck to give him access to all the sensitive places he touched. When his mouth left her skin, her eyes had drifted closed and her pulse was hammering so insistently, she wondered if he could hear it.

"Julie," he said.

Impatient with words, wanting him to kiss her, she blinked slowly, then reluctantly raised her gaze to his.

Still he didn't close the last gap between them. "It's a long walk back to town."

It took a moment to register on her drugged senses that he was offering her a last escape, with a chivalry that made him declare his intentions one more time.

She wrapped her arms around him, put her hand on the back of his neck, and lifted her lips to his.

His mouth came down over hers, hard, satisfying, and warm, slanting urgently to claim her, invading her parted lips with his searching tongue, penetrating the inner recesses of her mouth with the heat of raw passion.

Julie welcomed it. A fierce, possessive ecstasy blossomed deep inside her, and when Tanner broke the kiss, lifting his mouth from hers, she was trembling. His breath came harsh against the side of her face as he threaded his fingers into her hair and pulled her head toward his shoulder, holding her hard against him for a moment. She realized, in wonderment, that he, too, was fighting for control.

For the first time since she'd come back to him, Julie let herself feel the heady sense of feminine power that made this man tremble with wanting her. She lifted her head, moving against him, and pressed her lips against the edge of his jaw.

Tanner made a sound deep in his throat. His lips came down on hers again in a hard kiss, a wild, unfettered blending of tongues and mouths that sought full intimacy. His arms tightened on her, then raked down her back and her waist and caressed the curve of her hips. Julie melted against him, feeling the heat rise in her body as his strong hands kneaded her feminine curves. Her skirt billowed as he lifted the soft material around her hips, then cupped her buttocks and lifted her against his thighs.

He was hard, blatantly aroused, and he held her against him as if to make sure she knew the full extent of his desire.

Against his lips, she let her mouth curve in a slow, passion-heavy smile. "I'm not walking away, Tanner," she murmured, the words muffled and husky.

She felt his mouth curve against hers. "Good. Because I'm in no shape to chase you."

Laughter bubbled up from somewhere deep inside her, hardly connected to their words, stemming from the fierce, passionate elation Tanner had set free within her . . . that she had set free within herself. "You're a rider, not a roper, cowboy."

Smiling, still kissing her and holding her with one arm around her waist, he walked her backward two steps, then leaned to open the camper door. He snatched something inside, then the door slammed, and his mouth centered on hers again. A heavy and warm object flopped against the back of her legs as he wrapped her in both arms.

Her bones were honey, her knees pliant as the soft folds of a blanket spilled out of Tanner's hands. He walked backward a step, taking her with him, and she stumbled, her boots unsteady on the gravel. With a sudden movement he bent and picked her up, turning toward the grassy bank that led down to the stream.

"Tanner . . ."

His heel slipped on a loose stone, and his arms tightened around her, cutting her breathless laugh into snatches of protest. "What do you think . . . you're doing?"

"I know what I'm doing." He grinned at her and kicked the blanket. "Trust me."

Near the bottom of the bank he slipped again, caught the edge of the blanket, and fell backward, chuckling, taking her with him, catching them both as the blanket tangled beneath him. He leaned on an elbow, hooking his arm around her neck to pull her down on top of him.

She braced herself, hands flat against his hard chest, as her eyes drank in the sight of his face, half-hidden by the hat he always wore, and which was still, improbably, perched on his head. "Trust you?" she teased, her voice breathy.

Tanner's smile faded as his eyes perused her face. The rustling of the Colorado cottonwoods above them joined with the liquid babbling of the water, and the teasing words hung between them, given more seriousness by the sudden realization of how little they had teased each other, how seldom easy, trusting words or gestures had come between them.

Trust me. He didn't say it again, but the phrase whispered through Julie's thoughts. To trust enough to put her heart in the hands of a rodeo cowboy . . . or if not her heart, her body.

Those hands now spanned her ribs and slowly, deliberately circled the bodice of her dress until his palms were pressed against the sides of her breasts, his thumbs resting in the hollow between them.

Her eyes slid closed and her lips parted as he cupped her breasts. He drew in a breath and held it for a moment as his thumbs stroked their inner curves, then paused at their crests before starting a slow back-and-forth caress that hardened her nipples and raised an ache of longing that dispersed the moment's doubts.

She slipped her hands inside his shirt, impatient enough to pop the snaps that restrained her, then caressed hard muscle, silky hair, warm skin.

With an inarticulate sound of need, Tanner pressed his hands against her breasts, pushing them upward and together as he pressed his mouth against them. His hat tumbled off, and his hot tongue flicked into the valley between her breasts while his hands kneaded and caressed, forming and reforming the shape of her beneath her dress.

"I've wanted to take this off you since the first moment I saw you in it," he murmured.

"You're taking your time about it, then." She ached for the touch of his hands and his lips on her bare skin.

"I've waited too long to hurry it now." Slowly, taking his time, he raised his hands until his fingers splayed wide on her shoulders, and his wrists pressed against her nipples. His thumbs hooked in the straps of her dress, then drew them down her arms until they dangled around her elbows, and the front of her dress fell an inch below the pale yellow lace of her strapless bra.

Tanner's long fingers circled her elbows, sending shivers up her arms while his eyes studied her flushed face, bare shoulders, the edge of lace across the swell of her breasts.

Julie's hands moved on his chest. She followed the arrow of silky hair down to his jeans, unsnapping his shirt as she went, then pulling it out of his belt. When her arms caught in the trailing straps of her dress, she pulled them free. The flowered cotton dipped farther.

Tanner reached for the buttons at the back of the dress. She leaned away from him, then rose to her knees to pull the dress out from under her. He tugged it over her head, and a cascade of yellow flowered cotton billowed behind her as he tossed it. He caught her around the waist and pulled her back to him so that she straddled his hips.

Tanner's strong hands circled her rib cage, then, with agonizing slowness, moved upward on her skin to cover the yellow lace cups, caressing with his thumbs, barely pressing against her skin through the lace. A flood of sensuality gushed through her, chasing inhibitions she thought had been an integral part of her, leaving her wanton and willing. She covered Tanner's hands with hers and pressed them hard against her breasts, letting her head fall back, face tipped to the blue Colorado sky dappled by heart-shaped green and silver aspen leaves. Her eyes slid closed over the image as Tanner kneaded and shaped her breasts, his long fingers plucking gently at her nipples until they hardened with sweet agony.

He gripped her sides and lifted her over him, bringing her breasts to his mouth. Holding her, he traced the edge of lace with his tongue, then gently bit the tip of her breast before he drew the lace-covered nipple into the warm, wet depths of his mouth.

Julie's breath sighed out in a drift of molten sensation. Her hands clenched spasmodically on his shoulders, as a low moan of need and want came from her throat. Tanner caught the top edge of lace in his teeth and tugged it down over her breast. Cool air touched her bare nipple for a moment before Tanner's warm mouth replaced it, and another spasm of desire coursed through her. She moved her hips against him, rocking in rhythmic response to the thrust of his pelvis against the most intimate part of her body.

With one deft movement he turned her around and unhooked the clasp of her bra, then dipped his head again to her breasts, pleasuring and exploring with hands and mouth as if he would taste in these passion-filled moments the knowledge he'd waited thirteen years to learn.

Julie's hands slipped inside his loose shirt, seeking the warmth of his hard, honed flesh in a gesture that she, too, had waited years to make, though she'd never let herself acknowledge it. Now the burgeoning emotion so long denied brought his name to her throat.

"Tanner . . . Tanner . . ." she whispered. "It's been so long . . . such a long wait. . . ."

He slid his leg between hers, pressing hard against the juncture of damp yellow silk and lace. "You're worth the wait, Jule," he murmured brokenly. "Even better than I knew it would be," His tongue dipped into the valley between her breasts, then traced the lower edge of one soft orb. "God, Jule, your skin is like velvet. Softer than velvet . . ."

Tanner's mouth traced a hot velvet path down the center of her rib cage to her taut navel, while his hand outlined her hip, her thigh, the back of her knee. He stopped at her boot top, cupping her calf, gazing down the length of her body, covered now only with yellow lace panties and cowboy boots. He sat back on his haunches, an easy grin on his face, then took one leg in his lap while she watched, propped up on her elbows, her hair tangled around her face.

His smile widened. "I always wondered if you made love with your boots on, cowgirl." He pulled one off, dropped it beside him, and took her other foot in his lap.

Grinning, she wiggled her booted foot against his lap. "Spurs and all?"

He pulled the boot off and flung it over his shoulder. It flew toward the stream, followed by Julie's laughing protest, and landed inches from the water.

"Are they the same boots you had thirteen years ago?" he asked her.

"Yes."

"You haven't worn 'em much—for a cowgirl."

"I haven't done a lot of things much."

Tanner's teasing grin faded into a question, and his eyes flicked toward her face. Suddenly self-conscious under his scrutiny, Julie pushed herself up and reached toward him. "Now you." She quickly unfastened the silver belt buckle, flamboyantly embossed with a bucking horse and cowboy, then unsnapped the waist of his jeans. But her fingers slowed as they trailed down the hard ridge beneath the denim.

Tanner's hand covered hers, pressing her palm flat against him, guiding her hand up and down again while he sucked in a breath and closed his eyes. When he met the banked fire in her gaze, he swallowed and spoke in a voice hoarse with emotion.

"Boots or not, I want you, Julie. I wanted you the first time I saw you, and I never stopped wanting you. When you walked into that bar, Jule, I swear I could've been twenty-two again. I didn't dare touch you."

Beneath her hand she could feel the heat of his desire, and his words burned through her, arousing an equal-measure heat that had been banked for years but now smoldered, building, so that she couldn't in that moment understand how she had ever denied it. "Touch me now, Tanner," she whispered. Her untrapped hand played across his muscled chest and pushed the shirt from his shoulder. His mouth caressed the hollow at the base of her neck, and he shrugged one arm carelessly out of the shirt to thread his fingers into her hair and tilt her head against his seeking mouth.

When she pressed her palm against his jeans, letting herself explore the intimacy that still seemed only half-real, he caught a breath, tensed for a moment, then gently drew her hand away. "Not for a minute, Jule. I want you too much."

He shrugged out of his shirt, dropping it carelessly on the ground beside them as he caught Julie's unashamedly hungry gaze roving over his chest, following the line of silky, dark hair that narrowed down to the unbuttoned jeans. He pulled off a boot, dropped it, and reached for the other, his movements slow and mesmerizing. His hands stilled, and an expression of wonderment appeared on his face. "You're so damn beautiful, Jule, like that . . . watching me. I used to dream about you watching me."

"I always watched you," she admitted huskily. She placed her palms on the grass behind her, her gaze never leaving his face. "Even when I knew I shouldn't . . ."

Tanner dropped the second boot and moved over her suddenly, lowering her to the blanket. "Say that again," he ordered, his mouth close to hers.

"I always watched you, Tanner."

He pressed his lips against the corner of her mouth. "Again."

"I always—"

His tongue slid between her parted lips, caressed the sensitive inner surfaces, then took her breath away as he kissed her with a wild, demanding passion that went beyond words. His hands slid down her throat and kneaded her breasts, then his mouth followed their path, trailing damp fire along her skin, suckling and caressing her nipples until he drew a hoarse cry of longing from her, and she writhed beneath him. He kissed a path down to her stomach, and lower, as his strong hands stripped off the yellow lace around her hips, and she lifted her buttocks to let him undress her.

His mouth touched her, hot, wet, and intimate, and she bit off the cry that came to her throat. He stopped, looking up at her, his breath warm against that feminine part of her body while his chest heaved.

"Tanner . . . please . . . I want—" She broke off, rendered inarticulate with the driving passion he stirred in her.

His fingers smoothed her legs apart. "Let me love you, Jule. Let me make you want me the way I want you . . . enough to die for it. . . ." The lambent strokes of his tongue followed his words, fueling the sweet fire in her body until she clenched her hands around the blanket and twisted it the way her body twisted beneath his ardent ministrations. She moaned his name as her body turned liquid and hot, longing, and ready. She grasped his head and cried his name again with feminine demand and passionate need. He raised himself to his knees, responsive to the tug of her hands, and knelt over her, unzipping and pulling off his jeans in one rough motion. He knelt over her again, while her desire-drugged gaze drank in the sight of him, and a flush darkened her cheeks.

Trembling and yet controlled, he let her look at him, until her brown eyes moved back up to his, then he reached out for her hands. He pulled her up and dropped onto his back on the grass, holding her straddled over him, his hands on her waist while she leaned forward, her palms beside his head. He groped for his jeans and fished a foil packet out of the pocket, and Julie moved forward to give him room. After a few moments his fingers grasped her hips and guided her onto him, filling her slowly, exquisitely, with hard velvet heat. Her breath caught, and she clutched his shoulders. When he held himself still, his eyes flicking a question to her, she let out a long breath and moved over him.

Pleasure rippled from their joined bodies, filling her, shuddering through her. He let her set the slow, driving rhythm as he thrust within her, drinking in her pleasure as much as his own, in a union that went soul-deep.

Julie was lost in sensation, in the brush of wind on her sensitized skin, the waves of exploding desire that drove her mindless.

Tanner rocked against her, and his hands squeezed her hips, holding her as he thrust with a force that she welcomed and rejoiced in. She rode him with the reckless abandon he showed in the rodeo ring. She was lost to all thought and feeling except the exquisite rhythm that pulsed within her and carried her higher, stronger, sweeter . . . until Tanner's strident breaths became harsh with his impending climax, and she arched mindlessly against him, driving them both toward irresistible heat.

He groaned her name, thrust into her with a power that lifted her whole body, and a wave of ecstasy broke through her with shuddering, devastating power. She gave herself to him in a rain of hot surrender, crying out as she felt his heat released deep inside her, welcomed, taken, returned.

And in that moment of lush glory Julie realized she had found again something that had been lost long ago.

She collapsed onto his chest, her cheek against his shoulder, her hands tangled in the damp, soft pelt of hair as her eyes drifted shut and the gentle, exquisite caress of his hands on her back and her legs drew a final shudder of pleasure from her body and a sigh from her throat.

The scent of bruised grass beneath Tanner's shoulders drifted up to her nostrils. She ran her palm along his arm, her fingers trailing on the ground he lay against. Smiling, she muttered, "You carried the blanket all the way down here for nothing, Tanner?"

"Yeah, I guess I did at that." His hand crept down to her buttock. "Maybe we should put it to some use?"

She chuckled. "I can't."

"I can't either."

His hands moved up her spine, then stroked the back of her head, and his voice, when he spoke, had lost its teasing smile. "It's been a long time for you, Jule, hasn't it?" It was a statement of certainty, not a question.

"Yes," she said after a moment.

"How long?"

She raised her head, studying his face, and realized the question was more than idle reference to a distant past.

There had been two men in her life after Buck—safe, secure choices who hadn't stirred her enough for her to continue the relationships. They had both been intelligent, successful, sensitive. Neither one of them would have asked her how long it had been since she'd made love with another man.

Neither one of them was Tanner.

She knew he'd had women. Tanner's life stirred enough public interest to make the research on it effortless. There had been a long-term relationship, she knew, with a divorced mother of two young rodeo riders.

The thought brought a sharp, unexpected edge of jealousy. Had he lived with her? Traveled with her? Been some kind of temporary father to her sons?

The implications of that disturbed her in a way that threatened the beauty of what they had just shared. She broke the gaze and lowered her head to press her lips against Tanner's shoulder, drinking in the taste of him, the scent of his skin, the natural sensuality that took her out of her convoluted, unresolved conflicts and brought her such elemental, simple joy.

"A long time," she murmured, turning her cheek against his shoulder. "There hasn't been anyone else that I . . ." She stopped short of saying *loved*.

She had loved Buck, once.

And for that pale echo of the fire Tanner stirred, she had paid dearly.

"Kiss me, Tanner," she said softly, murmuring in his ear.

If she had to pay again, she didn't want to regret any moments not taken.

Eight

"Sorry."

Julie glared at Nick Johnson's unrepentant back. The one word wasn't even close to being adequate apology for his underhanded manipulations, but the cameraman's casual attitude said more clearly than words that she wasn't likely to get anything else.

He stuck a length of masking tape on a film can, slapped his back pocket, then turned toward her. "Have you seen that red marker around here?"

Habit made her scan the littered motel room. She spotted the marker on his pillow and reached for it.

"So," he said brightly, "how about that interview with Danielson? You get him to agree to it?"

Julie's temper snapped. She flung the marker at Nick's chest and felt a small measure of vengeful if immature satisfaction as he juggled film can and masking tape to catch it.

"*No!*" she stated. "I didn't get him to agree to an interview!"

"You're kidding." Nick's face reflected puzzlement that was much too innocent to be real. "You had *all* afternoon with him, kiddo. Didn't you even ask him?"

"I'm not going ask him, Nick." Her voice held a note of quiet finality that made Nick frown. "And I'm *not* going to discuss my afternoon." She turned on her heel and moved toward the door, followed by Nick's assessing silence.

"Oh," Nick said, just before her hand touched the knob, "Skye called."

Surprised, she turned away from the door. "Skye called? *Here?*"

"Apparently she couldn't get an answer in your room, so she thought you might be here and got the desk to switch the call. Enterprising kid."

"What did she want?"

Nick shrugged. "No emergency. I think she wanted to go to some party or other. She had to have your permission."

Julie's sigh was a mixture of exasperation and strained patience. "She doesn't give up, does she?"

Nick indicated the phone. "She was anxious for your call. She said she couldn't go until you called back."

Julie dropped her shoulder bag on the nearest bed and crossed toward the phone. "She was right about that one, anyway."

Skye picked up immediately, obviously hovering in wait for the call. Her bright, hopeful "Hello?" was a little breathless, and her overly polite "Oh, hi, Mom. How are things going?" was a sure clue of ulterior motives.

"Everything's fine, Skye," Julie said. "But if this is about that party with the sixteen-year-old crowd, the answer's still no."

There was an irate silence, followed by, "I'm almost fourteen, you know! You can't treat me like I'm still ten years old!"

"Skye, that's untrue and unfair and—" Julie started, but her daughter broke in before she could finish the sentence.

"*You* do whatever you want when you're not home! You were out all afternoon."

Julie bit her lip and fought down the wave of guilt that Skye seemed to know how to tap into. "I'm sorry I wasn't in when you were trying to reach me, Skye, but I can't help that. I'm not always—"

"Nick said you were out on a date with a cowboy," came the accusing interruption.

Julie's gaze flicked to the cameraman. "*Nick* said I was out on a date with a cowboy?"

"Well, maybe he didn't *say* that exactly," her daughter conceded, but Skye's emphasis on the word *say* was full of innuendo.

Julie bit down on her temper. "Whatever Nick said or didn't say, it's not the subject of this conversation."

"Oh, fine. It's all right for *you*, but when I want to go to one single—"

"What makes you think," Julie cut in, "you can discuss my life with Nick, and then use it to get your own way, young lady?"

There was a reassessing pause as Skye took in the degree of her mother's anger. "I wasn't discussing—"

"And furthermore, I've already said no!"

When Julie ended the conversation and met Nick's eyes, his expression was that of a resigned, been-through-it-already parent.

"Skye *asked* where you were." He shrugged. "I told her you were interviewing."

"You *told* her I was interviewing a cowboy."

"She has a thing about cowboys, kiddo. Her father was one, remember? She drew her own conclusions about where you were."

"I don't need your opinions about Skye, Nick. And where I *was*," Julie said deliberately, teeth gritted, "was stranded at the Greeley Saddlery because you set me up and left me there. I notice you didn't tell my daughter that."

"You weren't stranded. I arranged for you to have a ride."

"Oh, yes. You just neglected to tell Tanner Danielson he was being arranged."

Nick smiled.

"You take some kind of prize for arrogance, Nick," she flared at him. "You think you can manipulate me and Tanner Danielson and anyone else you choose into following your personal script? Who do you think you are?"

He grinned at her. "John Huston. Sounds like it played too. Bogey and Hepburn, *African Queen*. Love in spite of all odds."

In spite of all her eminently justifiable indignation, Julie felt her face color. She opened her mouth; then, unable to come up with anything to say that would leave her with her dignity intact, she reined in her fury and snatched her shoulder bag.

Nick capped his marker and grinned at her again. "It's about time you fell in love, kiddo. I've been wondering when it would happen."

"Keep wondering."

He slipped the marker into his pocket, appraising her. "You wouldn't have slept with him if you weren't in love, Julie. I know you."

She dropped the shoulder bag and spun around.

"You are the most arrogant, presumptuous, manipulative, nosy—"

"But am I wrong?"

Julie stared at him, frustrated, angry, and utterly indignant at his complete lack of contrition. "Did you ever hear of the concept of privacy, Nick?"

"When you've been on the road as long as I have . . ."

She glared at him, and he trailed off, with a shrug of apology.

"Yeah," he said. "I guess this isn't the first time you've been on the road."

No, it wasn't the first time she'd been on the road.

"You know what I mean, then, about living in each other's pockets, Julie. You can't help it. And the first time you laid eyes on Danielson—"

"I don't want to hear it!"

Nick raised his hands, palms outward, in a gesture that indicated he would back off. Typically, he didn't. "You can't deny it, kiddo. You generated enough heat to fire up the strobes. And from someone who hasn't noticed a single hunk of male anatomy in two years—"

"Spare me the X-rated movie, Nick!"

"I'm not talking X-rated," he said levelly. "Although I personally think it's about time that sort of thing crossed your mind. I'm talking about emotional involvement. I'm talking about—"

"All right. I get it. *Emotional involvement.* The stuff that makes a good documentary."

"The stuff that makes a good—"

"*Life,*" Julie snapped at him. "I've heard the philosophy." She expelled a breath, closed her eyes, and let herself sink down on the bed. She stared sourly at Nick, silently assessing the truth of his words. She was thirty-one years old, with enough bitter experience behind her to dam up a river's worth of feelings, but Tanner Danielson had touched her, and she'd found herself as emotionally involved as she'd been at seventeen. "All right, I care about this project and . . . the people in it. Maybe I'm even a little . . ."

"In love?" Nick finished for her.

"I didn't say that."

"You didn't have to. You think you can go around falling in love and not have somebody notice?"

Julie stared at him, realizing with a jolt that she had thought exactly that. If she'd thought at all. If she'd had anything in her head that could be described as a thought after Tanner had leaned down and touched her elbow, on the steps of the store, and she'd melted like honey in the sun.

"What's to notice?" she said defensively. "I'm not seventeen. I'm not going to throw my life away for some random emotional need making a belated appearance in my psyche."

"Random emotional need?" Nick queried sarcastically. "As in . . . ?"

"As in things like this just *happen* on the road, away from home, away from"— she waved a hand at the phone—normal responsibilities. I should know that. It's an occupational hazard when you work on the road. Rodeo romance. Cowboys are famous for breaking hearts. I know where it's going. And at least I have a life to go back to when it's over. That's the important part."

"Is it?"

She frowned at him.

"It's not a trick question," Nick told her, mouth quirked. "Just a question."

• • •

Tanner threaded his way through the reporters and photographers still wrapping up the night's shoot. When he caught sight of Julie's back, he stopped where he was, staring at her for a moment, feeling a wild, sweet surge of heat. She was wearing a white shirt, snug blue jeans that clung to her curves, and the boots he'd taken off her four hours ago. The thought of taking them off her again, along with the jeans and the shirt and whatever-color underwear she had on now had enough kick to make his breath hiss between his teeth.

A strobe flashed near his face, and he shot a tight glance at a photographer taking the opportunity for a close-up. The man muttered, "Thanks," then, following Tanner's gaze, glanced toward Julie. Tanner suppressed a primitive, irritated surge of jealousy and made himself mutter something polite to cover it up. The emotion was one he hadn't felt with this kind of intensity in thirteen years, it was the kind of raging-hormone reaction Tanner didn't associate with maturity.

Usually.

Julie shifted her weight onto one sweetly curved hip, and Tanner felt a possessive heat tighten his chest. They'd made love again on the blanket, the slow, eyes-opened kind, but that was the only answer she'd offered to his question about who else might be in her life.

It wasn't an answer he'd been inclined to argue with. He'd wanted her too much. He wanted her too much now, maturity be damned. One afternoon hadn't been enough. He wasn't anywhere close to letting her walk away now.

Julie turned around, microphone in hands, when he made his way toward her and murmured her name.

"Tanner," she replied.

She'd showered and reapplied makeup, but the smooth gold hair still looked tousled, and the lipstick didn't conceal the slightly swollen fullness of her lips. There was a faint pink mark on her collarbone above the round neckline of her shirt, where his cheek had rubbed against her skin, while he was making love to her. Tanner registered a slew of feelings: satisfaction, possessiveness, the compelling temptation to trace the mark on her collarbone with his fingertip, soothe it with his tongue. . . .

"Congratulations," she said smoothly, politely, glancing around at the newsmen in the corral. "Another win."

"Yeah." As if they hadn't spent all afternoon making love. Tanner's gaze played over her face, then wandered down her body and back up. He watched her eyes flick toward the new hand-tooled leather belt he'd slung over his shoulder, weighted with the trophy buckle he'd won in Reno. Her expression held a bemused question.

She'd worn Buck's trophy buckles when she'd been Buck's wife. She'd worn city clothes when she'd first come back as a reporter. She'd worn yellow underwear this afternoon.

He shrugged the belt down to his forearm. "If you're going to dress like a cowgirl," he told her, "you need this."

She blinked, a little disbelieving, but in answer to his slow, intimate smile, her mouth curved, and a faint flush heightened the color in her cheeks. In her eyes he read the kind of thoughts that recognized what they'd been doing all afternoon.

Still, she made no move to take the belt.

He reached toward her and slipped it over her arm and up to her shoulder, settling the smooth leather over the edge of her loose neckline. His fingers lingered long enough to generate heat between his stroking touch and the warm silk of her skin.

Nick glanced toward them, his expression carefully bland, and Tanner returned the look. His anger at the cameraman had dissipated with the satisfactions of the day, but he wasn't ready to acknowledge Nick as an ally.

"You almost finished here?" Tanner asked, speaking to Julie.

Nick glanced at them again and waved one hand. "Go ahead. I'll pack up here. We're just about done anyway."

Julie shot Nick a glance Tanner couldn't read, but Nick shrugged, ignoring the undercurrents between the three of them. Julie hesitated a moment, her hand on the belt, then she picked up her woven straw bag and turned to go with him. He slipped his arm around her shoulders, hugged her close to his hip, and maneuvered them out of the press corral.

"Where are we going?" she asked him, with a sidelong look, as he kicked open the door to the arena and walked her outside.

"My place."

"Your place?"

"Uh-huh." He nodded. "I have this pan of leftover chili that needs to be eaten."

Her eyebrows rose a little. "And you just assumed I'd be hungry for chili at eleven o'clock at night?"

He grinned at her. "I'll help you work up an appetite."

"You take a lot for granted, don't you?"

His smile faded as he gazed down at her. "No," he said. "I intend to make damn sure it gets granted."

She slowed her steps halfway across the wide sidewalk, and Tanner stopped beside her, letting her appraise the intention in his eyes, watching her face for reaction. The brown eyes looked back at his, serious and a little troubled.

He turned her toward him, resting his hands on her shoulders for a moment. The floodlights outside the building's entrance cast her face in sharp, classic relief as she looked up at him. Most of the crowd had left. The few stragglers still coming out wended their way around Tanner and Julie with only passing glances. The night air was cool, brisk. He felt her shiver under his hands, and he wrapped her in his arms and pulled her against him, lowering his mouth to hers.

The kiss was warm, impatient, questioning and demanding at once, and when Julie opened her lips to his seeking tongue, he claimed what she offered with ardent insistence, pulling her hard against his chest and bringing her up on her toes.

He lifted his mouth from hers but held her a moment longer, staring down into her face. "I've been thinking about that and damn little else for four hours, Jule."

"So have I," she admitted softly.

He drew in a breath, and his hand closed into a fist at her back. One kiss and he was hard with wanting her so much. It didn't matter that they were on a public sidewalk. He grinned and said,

"Come on, Jule. If you're gonna talk like that, we have to take to the shadows."

His camper was in a shaded lot two blocks away. They walked in silence, hip to hip, the belt anchored on Julie's shoulder with Tanner's hand, its heavy buckle jogging against her side with each step.

At the door of his camper Tanner let go of her to fish out his keys and unlock the door, then he handed her in to the dark, intimate interior.

She stood in the near blackness, aware of him behind her, anticipating his hands on her shoulders and feeling her heart already beating faster at his expected touch. It came as the warmth of his palm between her shoulder blades, and she turned into his arms with a soft breath of surrender, putting her hands flat on his chest. She couldn't see his face, but beneath her hands she could feel the driving beat of his heart. His breathing was rushed and strident as her own as he ran his hands down her back to her waist. The zipper of his jeans pressed lightly against her stomach.

Pleasure and wonderment trickled through her at the thought that he had wanted her enough to come to her and claim her with the trophy from a winning ride. She smiled, running her hands over his chest, learning by touch that seemed more sensitive in the absence of sight. "So what happens when we take to the shadows?" she teased.

She felt his lips curve against the hollow under her jaw. "We have to work up an appetite, woman," he said, the words vibrating against her neck. "For chili."

She tilted her head to the side, letting his warm mouth stoke the ardent hunger in her body, delighted and amazed that the effortless intimacy they'd shared that afternoon was so easily called back. "I thought we took care of that." She smiled. "This afternoon."

"No. Not hardly, Jule." He walked her back a step in the dark, then leaned away from her, one arm still around her waist, and reached for the cushioned bench seat against the camper's wall. She heard the creak and catch of hinges, then Tanner sank back, and she tumbled with him onto the pulled-out bed. "We've got thirteen years' worth to take care of," he said, his fingers at the tiny buttons of her blouse.

And it was care that he took, undressing her with exquisite tenderness, touching, stroking, kissing her in the dark until she murmured her need and fumbled at the snap of his jeans.

She heard the impatient rasp of the zipper and brush of fabric as he pulled them off, and then he moved over her, into her, with her, filling her with desire so urgent, she felt him tremble with it, then taking her with slow, ardent heat to that hot, passionate hunger she'd felt already twice that day.

"Come with me, Jule," he murmured raggedly, threading his hands into her hair. "I need you with me."

She breathed a sound of assent that became a murmur of his name as he stroked deep inside her, cherishing her with his body, filling her senses again and again, until they shared once more that quickening rapture of spirit that knew no separate beings.

When it was over, he wrapped her tightly in his arms, gathering her against him as he rolled to his side. Holding him close, Julie let her head fall back against Tanner's strong arm while her lips curved in a smile. "Oh, Tanner," she murmured, "I *have* wanted this. I *have* wanted . . ."

"Me?" he said softly.

"Yes. You."

"I'm here for the taking, Jule," he said softly.

Her eyes drifted closed in the darkness as she drank in the reality of Tanner's arms around her, his body beside her on the narrow bed. "I know. I know it now. I mean, I thought this afternoon might be just . . . a fluke, maybe a onetime thing." She paused, searching for the words to describe her wonder that they were so good together, again.

He stretched an arm over her head, reached for a switch, and the small room was bathed in dim yellow light from a reading lamp. In the sudden illumination they studied each other's faces for a moment, her expression solemn, his pleased, half-smiling.

"I told you, Jule," he said softly. "This wouldn't be a onetime thing. Not with us."

She felt her heart swell with emotion she couldn't quite repress, despite the warning voices in the back of her mind that she knew would demand reckoning sooner or later.

But not now. Not here, with Tanner beside her. She propped her head on her hand, letting her gaze rove over the room. "This is cozy, Tanner. Not the way I would have thought you lived."

"And how would that be?"

"Oh, a Cadillac, top-class hotel rooms, hand-tooled boots." She grinned at him. "Cowboy heaven."

He played with her hair, letting it slip through his fingers. "Cowboy heaven," he repeated, smiling.

"And winning rides," she added.

Tanner's hand stroked over her shoulder and down the curve of her waist to her hip. He squeezed and leered at her. "Some rides are winners, all right."

She swatted his hand away. "And some cowboys will go to any lengths to work up an appetite for chili."

"Hungry, are you?"

"Have you really got chili?" she asked, with interest. "I'm starved."

He grinned at her, then rolled away, swung his feet off the bed, and in the same movement hunched in front of the small refrigerator and opened the door. Naked and unselfconscious, he reached for a pot and stood to set it on the stove, while Julie watched the play of muscle in his back, the iron-strong, graceful balance of buttocks and thighs. He leaned down again to the refrigerator.

"Beer?" he asked her.

The gesture sparked swift memories: Buck reaching for the six-pack he usually had beside the bed, drinking it warm if there was no way to keep it cold. She shook her head.

"Soda, then?"

"Yes, sure." She sat up to take the offered can of ginger ale, then, shivering a little in the coolness of a Colorado mountain midnight, reached for her blouse on the pile of strewn clothes and put it on. The belt and gold buckle glimmered against her jeans on the floor. She picked up the buckle and traced the embossing with her fingers.

The gas burner flared on the stove, and she looked up to see Tanner leaning against the counter, arms crossed over his chest, studying her, adorned with only a pleased grin. "You gonna wear it?" he asked.

Obligingly she gave him an impish grin and buckled it around her naked hips.

"I wasn't sure it was your style these days," Tanner commented. "But I see it suits you perfectly." He stepped toward her, leaned one knee on the bed, and slipped his fingers behind the buckle, next to her stomach. "You make a very . . . sexy . . . cowgirl, Jule." His fingers brushed across the smooth muscle of her abdomen.

"Is that why you gave it to me?" she asked him.

The corners of his mouth drifted down. "I gave it to you so you wouldn't wear anyone else's." He held her eyes for a moment, then moved off the bed and pulled on his jeans. He zipped them without snapping the waist, then turned to the pot of chili.

Julie sipped her soda, her eyes following his movements, taking in the sight of his half-naked body, her mind sifting through memories that each carried a different emotion. "I used to wear Buck's trophy buckles for that reason," she said quietly.

Tanner glanced toward her.

"So he'd be reminded he was spoken for." A strained laugh followed the statement. "I'm not sure it always worked."

Tanner said nothing, and as he turned back to the stove Julie wondered if that silence represented damning comment about Buck.

Some of the old rules still held, she realized. Tanner would say nothing disloyal to Buck, just as he would never have touched her when Buck was her husband. He'd let her pretend back then that they were antagonists in order to keep the distance between them. Her brows drew together in a frown. How little she'd really known about him.

"Who'd you give your trophies to then, Tanner?"

"No one."

"But you must have had—"

"No one like you," he said. He studied her face a moment, his expression intent, then he glanced down at the buckle lying against her stomach, and she felt the heat of his gaze as if he had touched her.

Unsettled by her turbulent feelings, she looked away. "Maybe you should dish up that chili, cowboy. It's getting late, and we both have a long drive tomorrow."

"I'll drive," he put in. "You can sleep in the back."

"I can—" She broke off, glancing around at the back of the camper while she absorbed the idea that Tanner intended her to ride with him. "But what about Nick?"

He reached for a bowl and ladled the chili into it. "You can call him in the morning and remind him he owes you one. I have a feeling Nick's going to be accommodating."

Julie watched him put the chili on the table, set out forks, find a package of tortillas in the cabinet, doing the simple domestic tasks Buck would have considered beneath him. But Tanner had the kind of innate assurance that didn't depend on what he did, be it winning rides, facing down antagonists, or setting a table.

When he turned toward her, grinned, and muttered, "You still hungry?" she found that she was, and for nothing as simple as chili.

She was hungry for the experience of traveling with him, learning his habits and his faults and his fancies. She'd argued with him, laughed with him, made love with him, and he'd become more than a piece of her past.

Emotionally involved. She shut her eyes, still

seeing him against her closed lids, and admitted it. Nick was right. She was emotionally involved. In the project, in the life she'd temporarily taken up, in Tanner Danielson. He'd become a driving, irresistible part of her present, of her emotions, of her—

She stopped short of saying of her heart. For that implied that he'd be part of her future, something she couldn't count on.

Nine

Whatever fates governed the rodeo circuit seemed disposed to give Tanner and Julie time to learn about each other in the days that followed. Tanner's rodeo schedule—from Greeley, Colorado; Cody, Wyoming; Red Lodge, Montana, to Toppenish, Washington—coincided with her own.

True to his word, Tanner drove all the miles from Greeley to Cody without Julie's help, but the Rockies were too stunning to sleep through. As they wound their way through rugged snowcapped peaks and valleys verdant with evergreens and silvery-leaved quaking aspens, Julie sat beside him in the cab. Tanner's hand touching her shoulder when they rounded a forested slope and saw the Shoshone Valley open beneath them, the river rushing through it, was a sharing of spirit as important in its way as the physical sharing that had brought them together the night before.

Julie climbed out of the camper in Cody, stiff from the long ride and fortified only with coffee and takeout sandwiches two hours earlier. She planted her palms on the small of her back and arched to stretch out the kinks, then felt Tanner's hands on her shoulders, massaging her travel-stiff muscles with strong, expert pressure.

"Mmm . . . that's heaven." She let her head drop back and closed her eyes against the impossibly blue sky.

"You and Nick need a hand with the equipment?" Tanner offered.

She tipped her neck against his thumbs and smiled. "I don't know. Do I have to carry your saddle in return?"

He squeezed her shoulders and muttered, "No. You ride later, cowgirl. And you won't need a saddle."

That evening, at the end of the rodeo, Julie caught a grin and a jaunty wave from one of the stockmen she'd encountered behind the Lehi stock pens.

"You're getting to be a familiar face," Tanner commented at midnight over bacon and eggs.

"I'd find it easier to believe he won twenty-five dollars by betting on us."

Thoughtful, Tanner took a sip of coffee and muttered, "That all?"

"I wouldn't know."

He smirked behind the cup. "Hell, I won a lot more than that myself."

Caught between outrage and amusement, she raised her eyebrows, not sure whether he was teasing.

"And I've got a double-or-nothing going. Let's see," he commented with lazy innocence. "It's Wednesday. How many times have we . . . ?"

His eyes held a hint of mischief. "A couple more, and I'd—"

"Quit smirking, cowboy," she scolded him. "Or count your losses."

His smirk didn't quit, but there were no losses that night.

The following morning Julie cooked breakfast for him. Mixing pancakes in the tiny kitchen, she found herself smiling at the thought of Tanner in these miniature surroundings. "This is like living in a dollhouse," she teased him. The words *Skye would love it* were on the tip of her tongue, but Tanner's swat on her backside and mock leer kept her from making the slip.

"C'mon, doll," he growled in her ear. "Let's check out the shower."

But the shower proved too small for even the most inventive technique, and they ended up on the bed with their clothes strewn across the table and the breakfast coffee perking to black mud.

Two hours later, while she was checking the stock pens for Piece O'Cake, Julie was interrupted by one of the stockmen hollering, "Tell Tanner his ride's been pushed back," as he hurried toward the chutes. She realized, nonplussed, that they'd become an established couple. It had happened with the swift, inevitable flow of a well-scripted film, but the easy intimacy they'd discovered didn't go below the surface, Julie knew. And beneath the smooth current were snags and eddies that hadn't been tested.

Her partner's casual, no-comment attitude seemed the soul of live-and-let-live tolerance, but the cameraman's uncharacteristic tact made Julie suspect ulterior motives. And in Red Lodge, when Nick asked her casually if she needed extra tape for her recorder that night, her suspicions hardened.

"No," she told him curtly. The evidence that Nick was still waiting for an interview with Tanner made her tense and tight-lipped enough for Tanner to notice.

He leaned back in his seat, watching her pick at the pizza they'd ordered for dinner, folded his arms behind his head, and contemplated her. "Nick giving you a hard time?" he said out of the blue.

The astute guess made her look up guiltily, although Nick's machinations were nothing she herself should feel guilty about. But Tanner guessing more than she told him brought a sinking hollow feeling to her stomach that roused her conscience for not telling him about the daughter she would be going home to see in a few days.

Assuaging her guilt with the decision to be truthful about Nick, at least, she met his gaze and said, "He still expects an interview, Tanner. That's what he wants—for you to go on tape and answer all questions—and he doesn't believe I'm not coercing you into it."

"Is that what *you* want?" Tanner asked her.

She studied his face, feature by feature: the strong, stubborn jaw, the mouth that teased so readily and kissed with such tenderness, the serious blue eyes that rested steadily on hers.

If she said yes, he would do it, she thought, with insight that brought an odd flash of anxiety. He would trust her with a public disclosure of his history. He would give her honesty and straight dealing, and rely on her not to misuse it.

One more reason why he deserved the same from her.

Tell him, a small voice from the bottom of her

soul urged, but the thought of how he would judge her dishonesty closed her throat. She wondered, too, if he'd believe her purpose in telling him now was to pressure him into returning the favor on videotape.

Her shoulders tense, she folded and refolded the lid of the pizza box, looking down at it unseeingly. "You don't have to turn into a TV star for me, Tanner. You don't . . . owe me anything."

Her eyes flickered up to his face and unsettled by his probing gaze, she looked down again at her hands. He reached to cover them with the gentle pressure of his own. "I just asked if you wanted it, Jule. It's something I could give you."

"Tanner, I . . ." Her throat was too tight for her to say more, and the well of emotion that filled her chest at his offer moved her as nothing ever had save the love of her daughter.

Julie looked away, her sense of guilt making her feel unworthy and small. She wondered if he would demand a reckoning.

But he didn't. His eyes played over her averted face, then he murmured with understanding that tugged at her sense of honor. "I wasn't talking about paying debts, cowgirl."

"I know, Tanner. I . . ."

"Come here," he said gruffly. "I'll show you what I owe you."

She was late getting back to the press corral.

Even so, she took the time to call Skye from a pay phone in the rodeo arena. It hadn't been the right time to tell Tanner about her daughter, she rationalized. She couldn't bring up the subject just before he had to ride. And, she argued with her conscience, she had to tell Skye about Tanner first. Surely family loyalty demanded that.

But family loyalty seemed lacking in the phone call. Rosa's report that she'd found in Skye's pocket a roll of photo-booth snapshots of Skye and a teenage cowboy had Julie's stomach in knots. "What does he look like?" she asked Rosa.

The grandmotherly voice held more opinion than the words. "Sullen," Rosa said. "With cigarettes in his shirt pocket."

Skye didn't deny that Gary had walked her home from school one day, and what was wrong with that? Or did her mother object to *walking* now?

At the end of the call Julie's temper was frayed, and her loyalty torn to shreds between Tanner and her daughter. She squeezed her eyes shut, wishing for an aching moment that she had been honest from the beginning. She put the receiver back on the hook and leaned her forehead against it, sighing. She'd be home in a few days. Surely the truth could wait four days, couldn't it?

But her other life seemed to intrude between her and Tanner, where it hadn't before, as if bringing up the topic of Nick's expectations had opened a door to the deeper issues of dishonesty and pretense between them. Julie felt the weight of it like a black ghost of the past. On the six-hour drive to Toppenish, Julie sensed Tanner's gaze resting on her with a seriousness that carried unasked questions. Staring out at the passing miles, she rehearsed the answers in her mind, but no rearrangement of the words made them any less damning.

Tanner, before Buck died, I got pregnant to try to save our marriage, even though by then I didn't really believe it was worth saving. Now I have an

*adolescent daughter I don't understand, and I'm
afraid to tell her the mistakes I've made and
terrified she'll make the same ones.*

Staring across the cab of the camper at Tanner,
she felt all the weight of her secret, but she kept
her silence.

The Toppenish Pow Wow and Rodeo was on
Julie's and Nick's schedule for its traditional Native American dance and photogenic ambience as
well as the cowboys' contest. Nick's enthusiasm
pushed Julie's guilt to the back of her mind, but
Nick brought it forward again with a single, unexpected question.

"Why don't you bring Skye for tomorrow's rodeo?" he asked. "Have Rosa put her on a bus. You
could meet her in Yakima."

The idea surprised her. "No," she said quickly,
shaking her head. "I don't want Skye . . ."

"What? Watching rodeos?"

Julie hesitated, hearing the absurdity of Nick's
question, realizing that her fingers had gone to
the trophy buckle she wore on her belt. "Skye
doesn't need to have her life disrupted, Nick," she
said, knowing it sounded weak.

"A couple hours' bus ride? She'd love it. She
could watch Tanner win tomorrow." He adjusted
the focus on his lens and trained the camera at a
group of Native American dancers rehearsing beside the rodeo grounds, but at Julie's lengthy
silence, he stopped taping and frowned at her. "Let
me get this straight, kiddo. You don't want to
bring Skye tomorrow to the rodeo."

"Nick, I—"

"Or you don't want her to see Tanner ride?"

Julie shrugged, thinned her lips, and said nothing.

Nick didn't let it pass. "This is the project you're spending six weeks of your life on. And Danielson's the cowboy we're filming," he said deliberately. "The major talent for this project, the one who's slated to win the title, a guy you're supposed to be cultivating . . . and you won't bring your cowboy-crazy daughter to see him ride?"

"I'm not *cultivating* him, Nick," she muttered, conscious of the interested bystanders around them.

"Well, why the hell not? You obviously get along with him. You just spent six hours in his truck driving across Washington. We've got a project going here."

"I didn't drive across Washington to get an interview! If you wanted a partner with no scruples, Nick, you should have picked someone else. This project is not the only thing that matters to me!"

He stared at her, eyes narrowed. "You haven't told her, have you?" At her deep breath his voice became even more condemning. "You haven't told her about you and Tanner."

She met his gaze with stony silence.

Nick gave a cynical huff of laughter. "And you're bringing up the subject of scruples?" he asked sarcastically.

"I told you how I felt about the inter—"

"And that's a lot of self-righteous bull, *partner*. You're lying to your daughter, lying to the talent, and lying to yourself. So much for your scruples."

Julie clenched her jaw to keep her voice level. "I'm doing what I think is best, Nick."

"For your *personal* comfort."

"That's right! My personal life comes first. My daughter comes first."

"What happens when she finds out?" Nick challenged. "You going to keep this a secret forever?"

"It's none of your business, Nick."

"And none of Skye's?"

Julie pushed back her hair in a frustrated gesture. "What good would it do to tell her?" she burst out, agitated. "She has enough ideas of her own without seeing something she can misinterpret in her mother."

"Misinterpret?"

"Dammit, I don't like being secretive! But I'll do what I have to to protect my daughter. And I don't need your advice on it!"

Nick huffed again and raised his index finger toward Julie's face. "You sure as hell need someone's advice, kiddo. Maybe I can't tell you how to treat your daughter, but I have something to say about this project. And I don't like the way you're playing the cowboy who's the main talent for it, Fielding.

"And I have a real strong sense he's not gonna like it either."

Julie promised herself she'd tell Tanner immediately, the next time she saw him, but somehow, just as the moments for truth had slipped away up to now, they seemed to slip away whenever she reminded herself of her resolve.

And as the time approached when she planned to take a few days off from the shooting to go home to Seattle, the tension between them at her unbroken silence grew like the danger of a penned, angry bull.

She thought more than once she would have welcomed some accidental slip that would give away her secret, and, like the horror of getting what you wish for and finding it a disaster, the moment, when it came, brought not relief but panic.

Some of the newsmen in the press corral had caught on that Julie was a good source of information about Tanner. When *Rodeo Times* starting quizzing her about her "long-term plans" with Tanner, she realized, with horror, that the reporter was treating them as a gossip item, and the man's knowing smirk and sexist remark about Tanner's notable success with women fueled her anxious anger.

All evening she stewed about it, one moment telling herself *Rodeo Times* would never print such a trifling piece of gossip, the next moment picturing rodeo-crazy Skye reading the story in Seattle.

When Tanner grinned at her from the arena the following afternoon, she felt the reporter's eyes watching the exchange, and her answering smile could have cracked her face. When he climbed over the rails at the end of the events, waded through the news crew to get to her and put his hand on her waist, she stiffened, brushed past him, and strode out of the corral at a pace just short of dashing out. Tanner caught up to her halfway to the exit, gripped her shoulder, and spun her around toward him.

"What the hell's the matter?" he muttered as she glared at him, jaw set.

"Your reputation!" she shot back, lashing out in irrational anger because it was the only outlet for the tension between them. "And every damn cowboy who decided to bet on it, and the whole macho rodeo circuit's attitude that women are nothing but the spoils of battle."

"What has that got to do with me?"

Nothing, and she knew it. But her outburst was a relief from guilt, and she latched on to it desperately. "Don't give me that dog-ate-my-attitude innocence, *cowboy*. You're the one with the reputation for getting any woman you want, as long as you're winning."

He swore under his breath. Julie broke free and started toward the van. He snatched her elbow and brought her up short. "Dammit, Jule, stand still!"

She had no choice, but she seethed at him.

"You don't hang a man for his reputation," he said reasonably. "And you don't accuse a man of something and then turn your back and walk away."

"You're denying it?"

"Hell, yes, I'm denying it."

"When I saw you that first night in the bar, you had two women hanging on your every word, not to mention other parts of you."

"So what?" he shot back. "I've got a reputation because I talked to a couple of women in a bar? I'm old enough for that."

"You've been old enough ever since I've known you! Thirteen years ago you had women all the way from Calgary to . . . to Mexico!" She yanked her arm away from his grip and stalked away.

He caught her again, his grip rough this time, and his voice taut with anger he hadn't shown until now. "You didn't know me! You didn't know a damn thing about me then, Jule, and you don't know much more now. That's the way you seem to want to keep it. I can't tell you why. But you've got a hell of a nerve accusing me of some damn crime I didn't know I was committing!"

"I've got a hell of a nerve? Well, *you're* the one with the reputation for it, in the arena and out of it! And you don't care, do you?"

"Why should I? There's a lot of things I care about, and my reputation isn't one of them." He stood nose-to-nose with her, ignoring the interested stares of the people milling around them. "I care about my life. My friends. Buying a piece of land someday." His grip loosened. "You," he said. "You can't tell me you don't know that."

Her anger drained away like water in a broken barrel, leaving only the underlying tension and conflicting emotions that had started it.

"Maybe you wish I was different than I am, Jule," he said more softly, his voice husky. "But you've got to know I'm in love with you. I don't know a damn thing about what you've done with yourself since Buck died. I don't know why you won't tell me, but I know how I feel, and you know it too."

She nodded, a lump forming in her throat, then whispered, "Yes." She swallowed. "And I know how I feel, Tanner." She reached for him, her hands trembling and almost hesitant. Then she touched him, placing her palms flat against his chest, her fingers brushing across his shoulders with a gesture that had nothing to do with reputation and everything to do with what they'd shared, person to person, man to woman. He ran his hands through her hair, studying her face, his own face unsmiling, so serious, and so dear to her. "Can I take you home with me, cowboy?" she murmured.

He slid an arm around her shoulder and walked her to her hotel and up the elevator to her room without saying another word.

But lying next to him in the dark after they'd made love, filled with the treasured satisfaction of Tanner's words, of their recent union, idly playing over the unnecessary argument they'd had, Julie was struck with the sudden, overwhelming realization that what he'd said had been significant.

You didn't know me then.

She moved her cheek against his shoulder, raising her head a little to look at his shadowed face. She knew him now. His honesty, his steady character, his . . . honor. With dawning certainty she recognized the truth, and when she did, it was impossible to understand how she hadn't seen it before.

"Tanner," she said softly.

His hand stroked her hair, and he looked toward her.

"You weren't guilty, were you?"

His hand stilled, and he frowned a little but said nothing. "The Mexican girl . . . it wasn't you, was it? It was Buck."

There was a second of tense silence, then Tanner's breath whooshed out in a long sigh.

Julie repeated the truth, her voice stronger. "She was Buck's girl."

"Yeah," Tanner said finally. "She was Buck's girl." He spoke into the darkness above his head, not looking at her, saying the words that were so damning to Buck in a voice that held no condemnation, as if long ago he'd resolved it. "She was a wild one. She showed up at a bar one night looking for Buck. She'd run away from home, crossed the border, and hitched up to Houston. Buck didn't know what to do with her, so he . . ."

"Got drunk," Julie finished for him.

"Yeah." Tanner ran his fingers across his forehead, slicking his hair back in the dark. "Someone had to take her home to her daddy. She was just a kid."

Julie swallowed a lump of emotion. *Just a kid.* A little younger than she'd been herself, then. Like Julie, she'd put her trust in the wrong cowboy, and Tanner had stepped in to put it right. "You were taking her home."

"Yeah." He let out a grim bark of laughter. "But that's not the way the border police saw it."

"Didn't she tell them the truth?"

"They didn't believe her. I guess she had a habit of telling lies. Her daddy thought she was just protecting her rodeo boyfriend."

"And Buck?" Julie's voice had hardened with bitterness.

He turned his head toward her. "Nobody thought it'd be any more than a fifty-dollar fine and some bad press. After the conviction it was too late to change the story. And anyway, Buck was . . . married."

Julie shut her eyes, as if she could squeeze out the unsavory truth. "So you brought the girl home because Buck was drunk, and you took the rap for him because he was married."

He didn't deny it. Both of them lay unmoving in the darkness, but Julie felt the clash of emotions with every nerve in her body. "Why didn't you tell me?" she got out finally.

"I just did." He braced himself up on one elbow, facing her. "I've told you everything you wanted to know, Jule. Even the part about Buck I didn't think you wanted to hear."

Her silence acknowledged it.

"I'll do it on tape if you want me to."

It was an offer . . . and a demand.

He'd gone to jail because of her. He'd spent six months of his life there because he'd been willing to protect her fragile marriage, and now he'd told her the truth about it because she'd asked. And she owed him the same honesty.

He hadn't demanded to know why she was going home for four days in the middle of a shooting schedule that obviously didn't encourage a break, but he was asking her now to tell him, and he deserved some answers.

She owed him the truth. She knew it. But somehow the silence she'd kept for so long carried its own weight, and she didn't know where to begin.

"Nick's the one who wants an interview," she said finally. "Not me."

The answer mocked the deeper meaning of his words, and she bit her lip as soon as she'd uttered it.

But Tanner's patience, stretched out far longer than she had any right to expect, snapped. He reached out suddenly and set her on her back, his hands gripping her shoulders, holding himself above her. "What do *you* want?" he growled.

She made a sound of surprise and protest, but Tanner's grip was relentless. "It's your turn to tell me, Jule. What your life is when you're not following rodeo . . . the phone calls you have to make every night in private."

Shock waves reverberated through her as she struggled against his relentless hands, but Tanner went on unflinchingly, his voice harsh.

"Who're you going to see for four days in Seattle, Jule? A lover? A probation officer? A husband?"

"N-no. No, nothing like that." His weight pinned her beneath him. Their naked bodies were pressed together as intimately as they'd been a few moments ago, but this time in anger. The panic she'd felt at the thought of this moment, now upon her, threatened to drive the breath from her lungs.

"A daughter," she blurted out. "I have a daughter."

Ten

For a moment he stared down at her, his face as shocked as she felt, then the frightening anger drained out of him. "A daughter?" He fell away from her, lying on his side, while he watched her, unmoving but for the dark pulse beating in his throat and the incredulity that wavered in his voice. "You have a daughter?"

She blinked against the moisture that pressed behind her eyes.

"How old?"

"Thirteen."

"Thirteen?" he repeated, incredulous.

"She's Buck's d-daughter," Julie said, her voice choked and unsteady. "I g-got pregnant just before he died. I thought it would keep us together. But . . . but it didn't work. I was a fool to ever think it would, and then . . ."

She had turned her face away and closed her eyes as tears wet her cheeks, but Tanner reached for her and turned her toward him. "Then he died and left you alone with a baby to raise."

She nodded. Her lips formed the word *yes*, but no sound came from her throat.

With gentle fingers Tanner caressed the skin he'd held so roughly a moment ago, his face showing compassion and a search for understanding.

The warmth of his hand, the gentle gesture, brought new tears. "I . . . wanted her to have some security. To know where her next meal was coming from. It was so s-stupid to get pregnant like that, and I had to make it up to her."

His hand cupped the back of her head as he murmured, "Shh. It's all right, Jule."

"I tried to tell you, Tanner. But I just . . ."

"Why, Jule?" She felt his hand tremble with the emotion in the simple question, and guilt at the way she'd deceived him thickened her throat. "Why couldn't you tell me?"

"Oh, Tanner." She hooked her hand on his wrist where it rested on her shoulder. "I didn't want to be a fool again. I didn't want it to be like Buck."

She felt him flinch, and opened her eyes to his face, regretting the unintentional hurt. "I should have told you, Tanner. I know. But it seemed like telling you would have been the same thing as lov . . ." She trailed off, for she sensed she'd hurt him again, when it was the last thing she wanted to do.

She reached across the space between them and touched his face with her fingertips, in silent apology and desperate plea for understanding. "Skye's been my whole life, Tanner," she said.

Tanner's strong, warm hand traced her neck, her shoulder, her upper arm. "Your daughter," he said, in a voice that held wonder as well as incredulity. "You and Buck . . . have a daughter. What's she like?"

"She's . . ." Julie hesitated, not sure anymore how to answer that question. "She's . . . a normal teenager," she finished.

"She look like you?"

"No . . . like Buck. Just like him."

"She looks like Buck." He touched her hair, then traced her cheekbone, studying her face as if to picture the child she'd had with Buck.

"What does she do? What does she like?"

"She likes . . . cowboys."

There was a surprised silence. "She follows rodeo?" Tanner asked.

"No. She has a . . . boyfriend." Her heart filled with the concern in his voice, the gentle, protective interest she'd hoped, so many years ago, that Skye might have in a father. But it was Tanner, not Buck, asking these questions, and Skye was thirteen years old, not a baby just conceived. Thirteen years old, almost grown . . . almost old enough to fall in love herself. . . .

"Like you did," Tanner said.

"No!" The word was sharp, and she repeated it again more softly. "No. It's not the same. Skye's not like me that way." But her protest rang false, and she realized with a sudden, debilitating shock of understanding that this had been her fear all along.

"What's that mean?" he said softly. "She's not like you that way?"

"Just . . . leave it, Tanner. You don't understand."

"I'm trying to," he said, with an edge to his voice. "You think she's too young for a boyfriend, is that it?"

"He's not . . ."

"Not the right kind of boyfriend?"

She swallowed.

"I know a lot of the kids on the circuit," Tanner said. "Maybe I could help out, Julie. Talk to her."

"No," she blurted, a touch of panic in her voice. She shook her head. "No, that would just make it worse. She's going through a rebellious phase. She's too rodeo-crazy as it is. You'd just encourage . . . I mean . . . you don't even know her. . . ."

Tanner's eyes searched her face, as if he were reading something he wanted to know and didn't like. "And will I?" he said. "Will I get to know her?"

"What do you mean?"

"Tomorrow night, you planning to make some excuse around seven o'clock so you can go call her in private, as usual?"

No words came in answer. She knew she'd caused him pain he didn't deserve, for instead of anger at her deception he'd shown only compassion, caring, and the wish to understand. But the implications of introducing Skye to Tanner, of Skye's recent rebellion, her unsuitable boyfriend, the hurtful distance she'd retreated to in the past few weeks, were all too much to explain in a simple answer.

Before she could sort out her own churning emotions, Tanner let go of her, sat up, and swung his legs over the edge of the bed. He bent to pick up his clothes, pulled on his jeans, yanked up the zipper. He stood facing her, his shirt bunched in one fist, his face tight. "You just intended to forget all about this when you finished your job here, didn't you?" The stark edge of bitterness in his voice cut at Julie's heart. "This was just a two-week fling with an ex-con rodeo cowboy, and maybe you can tape it for your documentary."

"That's not—" She stopped, drawing in an agonized breath. There was just enough truth in his accusation to make it impossible to deny.

He stalked across the room to his boots, yanked them on, then gave her a look she felt even across the dark room. "Well, I guess you get it your way, lady."

"Tanner, don't go. Please, let me . . ."

He jammed his hat on his head; then, still shirtless, walked out without looking back and slammed the door behind him.

Julie flinched at the sound, then stared, stricken, at the closed door, while silence closed around her like a convict's sentence. Loneliness welled up, aching in her chest and thickening her throat as she wondered desperately if she should throw on her clothes and go after him.

But he was too angry to listen, she knew.

And he had a right to be. Tears filled her eyes. She clutched the sheets around her, miserable and self-condemning, blaming herself with accusations far more harsh than Tanner's own words.

She *had* used him. She *had* hurt him. He'd told her he was in love with her, yet she hadn't trusted him enough to tell him she loved him, and in her lack of commitment she was no better than Buck had been, thirteen years ago, when he was consorting with a seventeen-year-old girl and letting Tanner go to jail for him because he was married and couldn't face his wife with the truth. As now, thirteen years later, she hadn't been able to face Tanner.

Guilt washed over her. Julie hugged her knees to her chest and buried her face in the sheet.

He was too angry to want to see her, she told herself. If she went to him at midnight, knocked on his door, he'd let her in, but it would only be out of obligation. The thought of Tanner acting once again out of obligation to her, in even the smallest act, was unbearable.

She'd wait until morning, when he wasn't so angry, to find him and apologize.

Shivering and miserable, Julie pulled the sheets to her chin, hugged the pillows to her face for comfort, and gave in to abject, heart-wrenching sobs.

Tanner's camper was gone the next morning.

The campground owner told Julie testily that the lot was paid up for three days, and cowboys who wanted to stay out all night were none of his business. His tone implied that he didn't think most cowboys would appreciate the inquiry either.

All too aware that he might be right, Julie resigned herself to waiting for the afternoon's rodeo. If she had to apologize in front of every cowboy in the state of Washington, she'd do it, she promised herself.

But when she checked the roster, Tanner's name had been scratched off. Nick, with one glance at her drawn face and the shadows under her eyes, didn't comment on her report that Tanner wasn't riding. When Tanner didn't appear on the evening roster, either, Nick took a long breath, contemplated his videotapes for a moment, then glanced up at her. "He'll probably be back tomorrow," he said.

"Probably," she agreed tonelessly.

But he wasn't. Nor was he at the Snake River

Stampede in Idaho a day later. Julie and Nick concentrated on videotaping the other riders they had followed.

Too remorseful to bring up the subject of Tanner with Nick or anyone else on the rodeo circuit, Julie threw herself into the work, finishing all the details she could before her scheduled days off. She drew up scripts, made notations on all the tapes they'd saved, noted the B-roll footage they still needed to fill in the inevitable gaps between interview tape and action, and scheduled time for shooting, interviewing, and filling in background.

She worked until she was too tired to cry herself to sleep at night. Nick watched her do it for three days before his natural sarcasm surfaced.

"You might be special-programs director, kiddo," he told her over the tape monitor at midnight in Idaho. "But if you burn out the retinas in your eyeballs, you'll have to work the rest of your life in black-and-white."

"I'm okay," she told him tersely, her mouth set into a grim line that invited no further comment.

Nick let the silence last just long enough to let her know he was contemplating it. "No you're not," he told her. "But I guess your eyeballs don't have a hell of a lot to do with it."

Julie clenched her jaw and ignored him. She *was* all right. She would survive, as she had in the past. But beneath her steely control was a hollow, aching loneliness that frightened her even more than the desperation she'd felt when Buck died.

What she'd called on to get her through that crisis was anger—justifiable, deep, and self-sustaining. Now she blamed herself. Tanner wasn't Buck. Tanner had treated her honorably, honestly, openly. He'd offered her the best of what he had to give, and in return she'd deceived him and refused to trust him, and hurt him deeply.

She couldn't even apologize, because he wanted so much to be away from her that he'd given up his best chances at riding for a week. As he'd once given up six months of his freedom to save her from being hurt by her husband's deceit.

She pressed her knuckles against her mouth and willed herself not to cry. She'd be home soon, she told herself. She and Skye would have each other, as they'd had before, and it would get better.

As Nick pulled up in front of her Seattle house and Skye rushed down the flagstone walkway to greet them, Julie's first reaction was shock at how much her daughter had grown in the past weeks. Although Skye's headlong bear hug brought a piercing joy to Julie's battered heart, her first experience of home promised little in the way of either peace or healing.

They had their first argument before Julie had been home twenty-four hours. As Skye barely picked at the meat loaf Julie had made because it was her favorite, she brought up a plan that had obviously occupied her thoughts for the past day: She wanted to go to the rodeo in Cheney.

"But Cheney is five hours' drive from here," Julie protested.

"So?" Skye's pale blond eyebrows rose defensively. "You said five hours a day is nothing when you're on the circuit with Nick."

Julie's dismayed explanation that she'd spent the last three weeks driving to rodeos and wasn't excited about doing it on her days off met with a sullen expression.

"Fine," Skye commented, her lip quivering. "I'll just stay home, then. That's all I ever do anyway, that's all I'm *allowed* to do! Everybody else will go, and I'll just stay home!"

"Everybody else?" Julie ventured with dawning suspicion. "Does this have anything to do with that boy you've been calling? Is he going to be there?"

Skye's mutinous silence gave an answer.

"What are you planning to do?" Julie went on, hurt that even on this short visit Skye was scheming to get away from her. "Sneak off and meet him when you went for popcorn?"

"Maybe I'm not the only one in this family who goes sneaking off! Maybe you wouldn't even notice if I did!"

Stunned, Julie watched her daughter burst into tears and run from the table. "Skye!"

A door slammed across the hall, echoing in Julie's ears like a gavel of condemnation. Dumbfounded at Skye's accusation, guiltily searching her mind for some way Skye could have found out about Tanner, Julie rushed across the hall to Skye's room, then stopped outside the door, uncertain. Skye's cold "Please go away. I'll talk later" defeated her.

Disheartened and feeling totally inadequate as a parent, Julie left the issue unresolved, telling herself conflict was normal with a teenage daughter, that Skye hadn't meant anything. But later that night, lying in bed behind her own closed door, Julie cried bitterly over the cruel irony that Skye had accused her of "sneaking" now, when she no longer had the opportunity. Tanner had walked out on her without listening to any explanation, and without leaving any way to reach him. He'd made her feel guilty and inadequate to deal with Skye, and for that she should hate him.

But she didn't hate him. She missed him terribly, painfully, with a piercing, seemingly endless misery. And though she'd chosen her daughter over Tanner, and lost him, she was terrified that she seemed to be losing Skye too. And she had no idea what to do about it. What did she know about her growing daughter's needs? She hadn't even recognized her own.

Despite her promise to "talk later," Skye seemed to have forgotten all about the rodeo argument the next morning, and Julie hesitated to bring it up and destroy the peace between them. The station called to report their delight with the news spots Julie had been arranging on her schedule, and there were hints about a favorable decision on the special-programs-director position that would have brought unalloyed pleasure a few short weeks ago.

Now, as Julie hung up the phone, the triumph was muted by her sense of loss. She who could manipulate words well enough to gain promotions on the job couldn't tell Tanner Danielson how sorry she was for not treating him honestly.

Skye's reaction, when Julie explained the call, was genuine excitement, and they made reservations at Seattle's revolving skytop restaurant to celebrate the possible new job. Relieved and grateful that Skye's moodiness was over, Julie offered to take Skye's favorite minidress to the cleaner that afternoon.

By four o'clock she was back with the dress. "Skye?" she called, kicking the door closed behind her and dropping a bag of groceries on the counter.

There was no answer. Julie frowned, walked through to the dining alcove, and found her daughter sitting at the table, her back to her mother and her shoulders stiff. "Skye?" Julie crossed to the table and pulled out a chair.

Skye had been crying. Tears were on her cheeks and a smudge on her chin, and the knuckles of one hand were scraped raw. "What's the matter, honey?"

"Nothing," Skye muttered through stiff lips.

Julie gazed at her, baffled, the dry-cleaning bag clutched in one hand. "But where have you been, Skye?"

"The Quik Stop."

"On Maple Street?" Julie stomach clenched. "Did you go there to meet Gary?"

"Yes!" Skye blurted out. Her lip trembled. "But you don't have to worry about that anymore. He was with another girl." Skye burst into tears, pushed herself away from the table, knocking her chair over in the process, and ran to her room. The slamming of the door made Julie flinch, but this time Skye's misery couldn't be ignored. Still carrying the dress, Julie crossed to Skye's door and knocked. The sound of sobbing was the only answer. Julie turned the knob and let herself in.

The room—walls, ceiling, doors—was plastered with rodeo banners and clippings from *Rodeo Star.* The bed Skye had thrown herself across was covered with a saddle blanket, and a western hat hung over the mirror. On the nighttable, beside the picture of Buck that looked so much like Skye, was a carefully cut miniature saddle with the motto SKYE AND GARY FOREVER pasted across it. Shocked, Julie stared at the room in disbelief. The dress she still held dropped to the floor, unnoticed.

Her daughter propped herself up on one elbow and wiped the back of her hand across her face.

"Is this all"—Julie waved a hand around the room—"because of that boy?"

Skye's eyes were brimming. "His name is Gary!"

"Oh, honey," Julie started. "I'm sorry."

"You're not sorry!" Skye accused. "You never wanted me to see him. He wouldn't have another girl if you'd let me see him. But you want me to act like a . . . a nun!"

Her throat thick, Julie took a step toward the bed. "You'll have plenty of boyfriends, Skye. You don't have to—"

"No I won't!" Skye burst out. "You don't ever want me to have a boyfriend!"

"That's not true, Skye—"

"Yes it is! I don't have a father, and I'm never gonna have a boyfriend!" She pressed the back of her hand against her mouth. "But it's okay for you, isn't it?" Skye burst out. She scrambled off the bed, brushed past her mother, and ran through the door, pushing it closed behind her. Julie whirled around to follow her, and stopped in her tracks.

On the floor was a clipped magazine photo of Tanner Danielson, blue eyes glinting from under his hat, his dusty chaps slung low on his hips. Lying half beneath it was a creased and faded sheet of paper. Numb, Julie leaned down and picked up the letter that had spent thirteen years in the bottom of her scarf drawer.

Dear Julie . . . If thinking about you could unlock this cell and put me in Wyoming, I would have been there already . . . whatever you do, don't blame yourself. . . .

Her fingers trembling, she glanced up from the

letter when she heard her daughter's footsteps cross the kitchen and clatter through the back door.

When Julie reached the porch, Skye was nowhere in sight. Julie scanned the backyard toward Rosa's house, then she let out a breath and headed next door, where Skye must have gone.

Skye wasn't there. Shocked speechless for the second time in the space of five minutes, Julie listened to Rosa tell her Skye hadn't come in.

She had to be somewhere. But Skye wasn't at any of the friends' houses where she could have walked to, wasn't on any of the blocks near home, or at the Quik Stop on Maple Street.

When Skye had been gone an hour, Julie called the police. Their polite, sympathetic, but essentially "wait and see" advice was impossible to take, and a minute later she was crying over the phone to Nick.

"I'll be right there, kiddo," he told her. Twenty minutes later he pulled into her driveway, with his van, his city maps, his clipboards, and his air of no-nonsense realism. But when he asked, "What happened?" Julie felt a wash of self-recrimination that threatened to undo her.

"Oh, Nick," she choked. "She's out there by herself . . . and she's so angry at me. She found the . . . letters Tanner wrote to me before she was born."

"Oh, Lord," Nick muttered brusquely, but he let her pour out her list of inadequacies as a parent, her fears, her guilt, and her faults.

"The question is, kiddo," he commented when she finally ran down, "what are you gonna do when she gets back?"

The issue was important enough to distract her

from her desperate imaginings. She pushed herself up from the table, wandered toward Skye's
room, and stood staring at it.

She'd somehow made it impossible for Skye to
talk to her about her most basic insecurities.
She'd made Skye ashamed of her rodeo posters,
made her natural curiosity and inappropriate boyfriend and thirteen-year-old's curiosity about her
mother's old letters taboo subjects. Skye's method
of communication had become acting out, and she
was doing it now. The letter Julie had dropped on
the floor blurred in her vision, and she sent up a
fervent silent prayer for Skye's safety.

Two hours after Skye left, Julie's prayer was
answered. Skye was back, bedraggled, woeful, and
clearly unsure of her welcome. "Hi," she muttered,
staring at the floor.

"Oh, Skye." Julie swept her daughter into her
arms and crushed her to her chest, while Skye
threw her arms around her mother's neck and
pressed her face against Julie's shoulder.

"I'm sorry, Mom," Skye's said in a muffled, tear-
ful voice.

"I know, honey." Julie's hand clasped Skye's
head, holding her as she had when Skye was a
baby. A burst of relief and gratitude swept through
her. "I was just so worried."

"I was just walking around."

"Didn't you see the car? We went out looking for
you."

Against her mother's shoulder Skye shook her
head. Julie heaved a long sigh, put Skye out at
arm's length, and held her face between gentle
palms. "I didn't know what had happened to you."

"I'm sorry," Skye repeated. "I'm sorry I made you
worry, and I know we had plans for dinner, Mom.

I'll . . . hurry up if you still want to go to the restaurant, and I'll take the posters down if you don't like them, and—"

Julie felt a rush of emotion. "You don't have to do that, honey. Of course you're interested in cowboys. Your . . . your father was a cowboy."

Skye blinked at her.

"Buck Fielding was a good rider, Skye." She watched her daughter's face, hearing her own words—the ones she'd never said before. But they weren't as difficult as she'd imagined. "I know he was. I watched him every time he rode. You can be proud of that."

Skye wiped her nose on her sleeve and watched her mother, her brown eyes wide. "He was . . . a good rider?" she asked.

Julie nodded. "Almost the best on the circuit." Her throat worked, and she smiled at her daughter. "You can ask anyone who rode with him, honey. You can ask . . . Tanner Danielson. He was your father's best friend."

Skye nodded, then looked down at her feet. "I'm sorry I read your letters, Mom. I know they were supposed to be private."

"It's all right, Skye," Julie said. "There wasn't anything in them you couldn't know. You see, Tanner was my friend too." She felt her throat close around the words. "A good one."

Skye's eyes brimmed again, and Julie swallowed her own tears, then wiped at her nose just as Skye had. "I have an idea, honey. It's kind of late to go out tonight, but why don't you come with me when Nick and I go back to the circuit? We'll be at the Calgary Stampede for a week. It's one of the biggest rodeos on the circuit. Every cowboy in the West will be there."

"Could I?"

Julie nodded.

"It's the biggest rodeo on the circuit?"

Julie nodded again. "Your . . . your father rode in it more than once."

Skye swallowed, then her arms were around Julie's neck. Julie hugged her hard, her eyes closed.

When she opened them, Nick was watching from the dining-room doorway, one eyebrow raised in approval. "Sounds good," he said, grinning. "Your mother's still got our schedule in her head."

"Can I really go with you, Nick?"

"Bring your cowboy hat," Nick told her.

Eleven

The Calgary Arena was ablaze with lights, dust, and the heat generated by a crowd that numbered in the tens of thousands. Tanner ignored the din of the spectators and swung his leg over the top rails of the chute. He rested his boot for a moment on the bronc's withers, just in front of the flat saddle. Piece O'Cake snorted, sidestepped, and slammed his flank against the metal slats. One of the stockmen jerked his arm out of the way and yelled.

"Easy, boy," Tanner crooned.

He needed this ride. There was a good chance he'd forfeited the championship by dropping out of the circuit for a couple of weeks at the height of the season, but title or no, it was a matter of the prize money now. He had a ranch to finish paying for. He'd been traveling hard, trying to make up the lost money and trying not to think too much about the other motive that drove him: He had a woman to forget.

He lowered himself into the saddle, muttered a

word to the horse, then raised his arm and nodded.

The gate of the chute swung open, Piece O'Cake catapulted sideways into the dusty arena, and Tanner Danielson felt the jarring contact from his tailbone all the way up to the ribs he'd cracked the previous month.

Over the noise of the crowd the excited commentary of the announcer barked through the PA. "Tanner Danielson, three times national rodeo finalist, top of the list before he took a vacation two weeks ago. But he's makin' a comeback, and if any cowboy can ride this animal, it should be Tanner . . ."

The horse came down hard, twisted, and flung his head low between his front legs, sending dirt flying. Tanner's hat tumbled off as he was thrown forward, but he flung out his free arm, recovered his balance, and gripped the saddle with his knees, matching the horse with pure stubborn grit and instinct, blocking out everything but the ride. Exhilaration shot through him. They were going all the way. He could feel it. A grin destined to break through at the sound of the eight-second buzzer started somewhere in his gut.

"This is a ride, folks! Let's hear it for this cowboy and this bronc!"

The noise of the crowd was rising. The bronc twisted and bucked, and Tanner caught a dizzying glimpse of the chutes, the stock pens, a sea of excited faces, a flash of blond hair the color of sunlight and honey, uncovered and gleaming in the bright light.

A bolt of recognition shot through him.

She was there.

He couldn't have said what instinct told him

that, but it hit him harder than the jolt of the
horse as it slammed its hooves down into the dirt
and bucked as if the devil himself were calling the
shots.

Tanner took the fall on his hip and rolled to his
feet, jamming his hat on his head, his eyes glued
to the press corral. A sympathetic and acutely
disappointed moan rose from the crowd, and the
PA squawked something that included his name,
but Tanner ignored all of it.

She was staring back at him, her hands pressed
against her mouth, brown eyes wide and steady.
He headed toward her without bothering to slap off
the dust of his clothes, and climbed over the rails
to the press corral, hearing none of the comments
of surprised photographers and disgruntled cam-
eramen. He stopped in front of Julie, feeling the
tension across his chest as if they were still in that
hotel room where he'd just made love to her, and
she hadn't cared enough to stop him from walking
out.

"What are you doing here?" The words felt like
sandpaper dragged over his throat.

She lowered her hand from her face. "I . . ." Her
lip was trembling, and she caught it between her
teeth, then started again. "I came to see you ride."

The catch in her voice touched all the nerves
along his shoulders. He had to clench his fingers
to keep from reaching out to her; the thought of
her pulling back was something he didn't think he
could take.

"I . . . didn't come alone, Tanner," she said.

He'd noticed the burly cameraman beside her,
but he kept watching Julie.

"I brought my daughter."

He stopped breathing, then moved his eyes from

Julie's face to the young girl she'd drawn up beside her with an arm around the kid's shoulders. A younger version of Buck, blond, brown-eyed, already beautiful, hunched her shoulders and sucked nervously on her lower lip.

Tanner let out his breath, and raised his hand to the brim of his hat. "How do, ma'am."

"Skye," Julie said to the wide-eyed girl, "this is Tanner Danielson, a man I've wanted you to meet."

"I know," Skye breathed. "I mean, I have your picture . . . oh, gee . . ."

The corners of his mouth turned up.

"You were a friend of my father's," the girl said, looking at him. "And . . . of my mom's."

Tanner's gaze met Julie's again, and he waited.

"He was, Skye. And he is now," Julie said quietly. "Even more."

Tanner could have been turned to stone. There was an island of restless, speculative silence around them. He was too used to crowds to give it any of his attention, but even if he hadn't been, no force in the world could have separated his gaze from Julie's.

Into the tension so thick it could have been roped and tied, Julie's girl murmured awkwardly, "I'm . . . sorry you lost the ride."

Slowly Tanner loosened his fists. "I didn't lose," he said. He reached for Julie with the intention of just touching her hair, but suddenly she was in his dusty arms, her own arms around his neck, murmuring his name in a squeak as the breath was squeezed out of her lungs. He lifted her off her feet and spun her in a joyous, exultant circle. Her clean, silky hair was against his cheek, and the remembered feel of her, smell of her, the warmth of her, were pouring into him like hundred-proof liquor.

He let her slide down along his chest and kissed her, long and hard and so intimately that he could feel the beat of her heart in time with his. She returned the kiss, telling him with that act what he'd waited thirteen years to hear.

When he finally lifted his mouth from hers, he felt himself grinning as he hadn't grinned in two weeks. Julie gave him back a smile both tremulous and joyful, then glanced at the young girl who was watching them with her mouth open and her eyes round.

Tanner let go of Julie, but kept one hand around her shoulders as he faced her daughter and wondered, for a moment, what to say to her.

"Skye," he finally uttered, "I'm glad to meet you. I asked your mother to introduce me."

"You did?"

He nodded.

"Why?" Skye said in a tentative voice.

"Because I wanted to get to know you. Because we have some things to talk about." He glanced at Julie, then back to Skye. "Because I want you both to see my ranch."

"See your ranch?" Skye echoed.

"Yes."

"You have . . . horses?"

He grinned. "A couple of dozen on a few hundred acres in Montana. A lot more next year, I hope."

Skye's gaze, so like her mother's, moved cautiously from Tanner to Julie.

"Would you like that?" Tanner asked.

"Yeah, I guess I would."

Tanner nodded, then his gaze moved to the face of the woman he'd been trying to forget for two weeks. The one he'd been trying to forget for thirteen years.

"Yes," she said softly. "I'd like that."

Behind and around them, the press crew shifted and murmured as the next rider came out of the chute.

"Here, kid," Nick muttered to Skye. "Take this mike a minute, will you?"

"What for?" Skye said.

The burly cameraman made a cynical sound in the back of his throat and fed another cassette to the video camera. "Because I have a feeling your mother and the cowboy want to talk. And we got a project to finish here, kiddo."

The night was clear and warm, the streets outside the arena bustling with cowboys, tourists, and rodeo-goers, all of them, it seemed, in western gear. Five steps from the exit Tanner stopped, swung Julie toward him, and leaned down to kiss her with long, hard, breathtaking concentration that made her head spin and chased away all thoughts of the crowd milling around them.

"I had to do that again, Jule," he muttered. "I couldn't wait any longer."

"Me neither." She tangled her fingers in his hair, smiling against his lips, feeling his grin curve his mouth.

"You couldn't have wanted it as much as I did, cowgirl," he teased.

"Want to bet?"

His answer was a muffled sound lost in a kiss, but his hands roamed her back, her shoulders, her hips, as if he hungered to touch all of her at once. Julie pressed against him while a fierce, heady joy swept through her.

"How long do we have?" he murmured finally.

"How long?"

"Before we have to go back to your daughter. Will she be wondering what we're doing?"

At the note of concern in his voice Julie's heart swelled to fill her chest. That Tanner should be worrying about Skye overwhelmed her. She laid her hand along the side of his face, blinking against the sudden moisture in her eyes. "She'll be okay with Nick, Tanner," she said softly. "She's important to me, but so are you. So are we."

He covered her hand with his. The blue eyes crinkled at the corners. "How important?"

"Let me show you, cowboy," she said in a husky murmur. "Where are you staying?"

"My hotel's a ways from here," he told her, kissing her again. "We have to take a cab."

"Where do we get one?" she murmured back.

Tanner broke the kiss, already walking as he tucked her into the crook of his arm and headed toward the cabstand. When he'd handed her into an idling vehicle, given directions to the driver, and pulled the door shut, he turned her toward him again and pulled her into his arms.

"You get a good score, cowboy?" the cabbie asked minutes later when they arrived at the hotel. He was smirking, glancing at them in his mirror.

"No," Julie told him, floating too high to be offended by the unchivalrous comment. "But he will."

"What kind of remark was that for a lady to make?" Tanner teased her as he walked her across the lobby.

"Honest," Julie told him, smiling.

They rode the elevator in silence, and Julie's smile faded as she glanced toward him to find him studying her, his expression solemn, his eyes level. They didn't speak as they walked down the corridor to Tanner's room, and when they were inside it, with the door closed, she stood for a moment looking around, her throat tight.

"Tanner . . ." she said.

He stood still, waiting for her to speak.

"I want to be honest," she continued. "I want to tell you I'm sorry, for not telling you about Skye, for being—"

Tanner closed the distance between them with one long step and cupped the back of her head with both hands, tipping her face up to his. "I know, Jule. It's all right. I know why you did it. I know how much she means to you."

"She knows how much you mean to me too," she said quietly. "I told her, on the drive out here."

Tanner's hands went still against her face.

"I think she guessed it anyway, Tanner. She found . . ." Julie hesitated, then lifted her eyes to his again and went on, "She found your letters. The ones you wrote to me after Buck died."

"The ones you didn't answer? You kept them?"

"I answered them a thousand times, Tanner. Just never on paper."

His hands tightened around her face for a moment. "How'd you answer, Jule?" he murmured, his voice gruff.

She didn't bother with words. She reached to pull his head down to hers, inviting his kiss, and when his mouth touched her she felt a sweet, hot rush of emotion that filled all the empty holes of the lonely past, that healed and forgave and carried the precious gift of new life to body and soul.

Tanner's hat slipped off his head and thudded on the carpet, while Julie's hands moved greedily against his dusty shirt, reveling in the texture of hard muscle beneath it, lost in the delight of her senses and the fulfillment of her heart.

"I love you, Tanner Danielson," she whispered, her face buried in the hollow of his shoulder. "I love the feel of you and the sight of you and the smell of you."

She felt the breath rush out of his chest in a single triumphant huff. "Do you really, Julie Fielding?" He held her away from him to grin down at her.

"Yes. Really."

"I smell like rodeo dirt."

"When you love a cowboy, you don't mind a little rodeo dirt."

"I hit the dirt because of you, you know," he told her gruffly. "I saw you, and it was all over."

Julie's hands stilled on his shoulders as her teasing smile became shaded with passionate promise. "Then I'll have to make it up to you, won't I?"

They undressed each other, slowly finding the intimacy they'd shared for a few intense, gilded days together.

"I thought about you every minute of the last two weeks," Tanner murmured. "I went crazy thinking about you, I tried everything I could to stop it, but nothing worked."

"I know," she breathed. "I couldn't stop either. I missed you so. . . ."

He swept his arm beneath her bare legs and picked her up, then carried her to the bed.

His mouth on hers was slow, gentle, expert, and his hands roaming her shoulders, her arms, the bare skin of her rib cage were sensual and seductive, caressing, relearning, claiming again the passion she'd given many times with such joy.

As she reveled in his touch, she took equal pleasure in pleasuring him, in the ripple of muscle across his chest, the sleek tendons at the side of his neck, the square bones of his hips and the magnificent velvet heat of his arousal.

"Ah . . . Julie . . ." he groaned, pressing her hand hard against him to capture his heat, though she offered no resistance, only wonderment at the sight of him, his head thrown back, his eyes tight shut in response to her. After a long moment he opened his eyes and looked at her. "I thought I'd never see you again, Jule. I thought you just wanted to walk out of my life after we were together, and I couldn't settle for that. I couldn't take being just a two-week fling. Not with you."

"You could never be that, Tanner, never. I love you. I think I did thirteen years ago, when I got those letters I couldn't answer."

"You can answer 'em now, Jule."

"Yes," she breathed, but her answer was lost in sensation and touch and wordless murmur as together they wove the sensuous, timeless spell that could free them from the past. She moaned his name deep in her throat and parted her legs to cradle him between her thighs, and he joined their bodies together in the ancient, primeval act of love that spoke a language before words, before time, before understanding.

Julie's body welcomed his, riding the powerful surges of his passion, matching his rhythm with her own, moving with him to that ultimate, timeless joining she knew had been inevitable since the first time they'd met.

They shared once again the shattering moment that dissolved all separateness, then drifted together on the melting, dispersing cloud of ecstasy that carried them down from the peak.

Julie's breath was a soft, moist warmth against his shoulder, Tanner's hand a gentle, slow caress on her back as they lay together afterward.

"Jule . . ." he said finally, his voice seeming dragged from the depths of lassitude, but with a teasing smile in the tone that she recognized as part of the ritual of their lovemaking.

"Mmm?" She moved her fingers on his shoulder.

"You hungry yet?"

She smiled against his damp chest. "Starved."

"We'll have to take Skye with us, huh? I suppose kids get hungry too."

"Regularly," she told him, smiling. "Then you finally get dinner ready, and they have to be called three times and won't eat their vegetables."

His chest rose and fell in a chuckle. "Raising a daughter doesn't sound easy."

"No."

He ran his hand through her hair, twisting his head to look at her. "I want to find out what it's like, Jule. I want to make this permanent. You know that."

She raised her eyes to his and studied his serious expression, then nodded. "I know. And the answer is yes."

She watched the slow curve of his mouth, feeling her own smile spread all through her body in response, aware of a surge of love that filled her as nothing ever had.

"How'll we do it?" Tanner asked.

"Nick wants to film the rest of the season—stay with the rodeo, follow it until the finals, make a two-hour special of it. He's been dropping hints since the Lehi Roundup."

"Could you do that?"

She nodded again. "I'd have to turn down the promotion they're going to offer me, take a few months' leave, but they'd probably keep my job open."

He considered her a moment, his hands moving again in her hair. "That job—that's what you want?"

She drew in a deep breath, then let it out. "It's what I've always wanted, but I've thought some-times on this project . . ." She sighed again. "I want to be honest, Tanner. I don't want to keep anything from you. I don't . . . know yet."

Tanner said nothing, willing to listen, giving her permission to say what she wasn't yet sure of.

"Nick makes a film every two years or so," Julie started. "He wants me to work with him. It would mean a few months of travel and shooting, then several more of editing, polishing, planning the next project."

"Can a person do that from a ranch in Mon-tana?" he asked her finally.

"I think . . . a person might be able to."

"Whatever you want to do, Jule, we'll work it out. If you want to stay in Seattle, I'll buy a ranch there." His hand stroked her back down to the hollow of her spine and back again, starting that slow, sure sensitization she would have thought was impossible so soon after what they'd just shared. "It'll work," he murmured, as if in answer to her straying thoughts.

Her lips curved in a smile. "In Seattle? A ranch?"

His hand stroked down again, drifting lower. "I'll park my camper in your yard. I've only got a couple dozen horses so far. I'll buy a ranch house and put 'em in that."

She raised her leg at the gentle urging of his hand, bending her knee as he stroked a slow path along her inner thigh. "What will the neighbors say?" she murmured, laughing.

"I don't care. What do you say?"

His hand reached its destination, then slowed and stopped, pressing gently against the warm core of her being as her eyes drifted shut and her breath sighed out again in pleasure.

"What do you say, cowgirl?" he murmured against her lips, his voice husky.

She said his name, and then a wordless sound of surrender. Her answer wasn't needed.

THE EDITOR'S CORNER

The coming month brings to mind lions and lambs—not only in terms of the weather but also in terms of our six delightful LOVESWEPTs. In these books you'll find fierce and feisty, warm and gentle characters who add up to a rich and exciting array of folks whose stories of falling in love are enthralling.

Let Joan Elliott Pickart enchant you with her special brand of **NIGHT MAGIC,** LOVESWEPT #534. Tony Murretti knows exactly what he wants when he hires Mercy Sloan to design the grounds of his new home, but he never expected what he gets—a spellbinding redhead who makes him lose control! Tony vowed long ago never to marry, but the wildfire Mercy sparks in his soul soon has him thinking of settling down forever. This book is too good to resist.

Fairy tales can come true, as Jordon Winters learns in award-winning Marcia Evanick's **GRETCHEN AND THE BIG BAD WOLF,** LOVESWEPT #535—but only after he's caught in a snowdrift and gets rescued by what looks like a snow angel in a horse-drawn sleigh. Gretchen Horst is a seductive fantasy made gloriously real . . . until he discovers she's the mayor of the quaint nearby town and is fiercely opposed to his company's plan to build new homes there. Rest assured that there's a happy ending to this delightful romance.

Terry Lawrence's **FOR LOVERS ONLY,** LOVESWEPT #536, will set your senses ablaze. Dave King certainly feels on fire the first time he kisses his sister-in-law Gwen Stickert, but she has always treated him like a friend. When they're called to mediate a family fight at a romantic mountain cottage, Dave decides it's time to raise the stakes—to flirt, tease, and tantalize Gwen until she pleads for his touch. You're sure to find this romance as breathlessly exciting as we do.

Janet Evanovich returns with another one of her highly original and very funny love stories, **NAUGHTY NEIGH-**

BOR, LOVESWEPT #537, for which she created the most unlikely couple for her hero and heroine. Pete Streeter is a handsome hellraiser in tight-fitting jeans while Louisa Brannigan is a congressman's aide who likes to play it safe. When these two get entangled in a search for a missing pig, the result is an unbeatable combination of hilarious escapades and steamy romance. Don't miss this fabulous story!

You'll need a box of tissues when you read Peggy Webb's emotionally powerful **TOUCHED BY ANGELS,** LOVESWEPT #538. Jake Townsend doesn't think he'll ever find happiness again—until the day he saves a little girl and she and her mother, Sarah Love, enter his life. Sarah makes him want to believe in second chances, but can her sweet spirit cleanse away the darkness that shadows his soul? Your heart will be touched by this story, which is sure to be a keeper. Bravo, Peggy!

Spice up your reading with **A TASTE OF TEMPTATION** by Lori Copeland, LOVESWEPT #539, and a hero who's Hollywood handsome with a playboy's reputation to match. Taylor McQuaid is the type that Annie Malone has learned only too well never to trust, but she's stuck with being his partner in cooking class. And she soon discovers he'll try anything—in and out of the kitchen—to convince her he's no unreliable hotshot but his own man. An absolutely terrific romance.

On sale this month from FANFARE are four fabulous novels. National bestseller **TEXAS! SAGE** by Sandra Brown is now available in the paperback edition. You won't want to miss this final book in the sizzling TEXAS! trilogy, in which Lucky and Chase's younger sister Sage meets her match in a lean, blue-eyed charmer. Immensely talented Rosanne Bittner creates an unforgettable heroine in **SONG OF THE WOLF.** Young, proud, and beautiful, Medicine Wolf possesses extraordinary healing powers and a unique sensitivity that leads her on an odyssey into a primeval world of wildness, mystery, and passion. A compelling novel by critically acclaimed Diana Silber, **LATE NIGHT DANCING** follows the lives of three friends—sophisticated Los Angeles women who are busy, successful, and on the fast track of romance and sex, because, like women everywhere, they hunger for a man to love. Finally, the ever-popular Virginia Lynn lets her imagination soar across the ocean to England in the historical romance **SUMMER'S KNIGHT**. Heiress Summer St. Clair is stranded penniless on the streets of London, but her terrifying ordeal soon turns to passionate adventure when she catches the glittering eyes of the daring Highland rogue Jamie Cameron.

Also on sale this month in the Doubleday hardcover edition (and in paperback from FANFARE in May) is **LADY HELLFIRE** by Suzanne Robinson, a lush, dramatic, and poignant historical romance. Alexis de Granville, Marquess of Richfield, is a cold-blooded rogue whose dark secrets have hardened his heart to love—until he melts at the fiery touch of Kate Grey's sensual embrace. Still, he believes himself tainted by his tragic—and possibly violent—past and resists her sweet temptation. Tormented by unfulfilled desires, Alexis and Kate must face a shadowy evil before they can surrender to the deepest pleasures of love. . . .

Happy reading!

With warmest wishes,

Nita Taublib

Nita Taublib
Associate Publisher/LOVESWEPT
Publishing Associate/FANFARE

FANFARE

Sandra Brown

_____ 28951-9 TEXAS! LUCKY .... $4.50/5.50 in Canada
_____ 28990-X TEXAS! CHASE .... $4.99/5.99 in Canada

Amanda Quick

_____ 28932-2 SCANDAL .... $4.95/5.95 in Canada
_____ 28354-5 SEDUCTION .... $4.99/5.99 in Canada
_____ 28594-7 SURRENDER .... $4.50/5.50 in Canada

Nora Roberts

_____ 27283-7 BRAZEN VIRTUE .... $4.50/5.50 in Canada
_____ 29078-9 GENUINE LIES .... $4.99/5.99 in Canada
_____ 26461-3 HOT ICE .... $4.99/5.99 in Canada
_____ 28578-5 PUBLIC SECRETS .... $4.95/5.95 in Canada
_____ 26574-1 SACRED SINS .... $4.99/5.99 in Canada
_____ 27859-2 SWEET REVENGE .... $4.99/5.99 in Canada

Iris Johansen

_____ 28855-5 THE WIND DANCER .... $4.95/5.95 in Canada
_____ 29032-0 STORM WINDS .... $4.99/5.99 in Canada
_____ 29244-7 REAP THE WIND .... $4.99/5.99 in Canada

---

Ask for these titles at your bookstore or use this page to order.

Please send me the books I have checked above. I am enclosing $ _____ (please add $2.50 to cover postage and handling). Send check or money order, no cash or C. O. D.'s please.

Mr./ Ms. _____

Address _____

City/ State/ Zip _____

Send order to: Bantam Books, Dept. FN, 414 East Golf Road, Des Plaines, IL 60016
Please allow four to six weeks for delivery.
Prices and availablity subject to change without notice.   FN 16 - 12/91